DROW CONQUEROR

DROW CONQUEROR

ALISON BROWNSTONE™ BOOK FOURTEEN

JUDITH BERENS   MARTHA CARR   MICHAEL ANDERLE

DISRUPTIVE IMAGINATION®

THE DROW CONQUEROR TEAM

Thanks to the JIT Readers

Dave Hicks
Diane L. Smith
Deb Mader
John Ashmore
Charles Tillman
Jeff Eaton
Peter Manis
Shari Regan
Nicole Emens
John Raisor
Jeff Goode
Dorothy Lloyd
Paul Westman

If we've missed anyone, please let us know!

Editor
SkyHunter Editing Team

DEDICATIONS

From Martha

To everyone who still believes in magic
and all the possibilities that holds.
To all the readers who make this
entire ride so much fun.
And to my son, Louie and so many wonderful friends who
remind me all the time of what
really matters and how wonderful
life can be in any given moment.

From Michael

To Family, Friends and
Those Who Love
To Read.
May We All Enjoy Grace
To Live The Life We Are
Called.

CHAPTER ONE

Alison grimaced and placed her hand over the throbbing hole in her shoulder. Dark tendrils of shadow filled the wound, and the pain began to fade. She'd let herself get a little cocky despite the shower of anti-magic bullets, but the round had passed easily through her body and jerked her back to reality. Thankfully, it was a clean and simple injury.

"One week back from my honeymoon, and this is happening," she shouted and shook her fist at the sky. "Thanks, Latherby, for this wonderful trip to San Francisco. So much history, interesting sightseeing, and heavily equipped mercenaries who don't know when to give up."

Hana shook the blood off her *tachi* and sheathed the sword. She'd already deactivated her defensive ring. "Think of it this way—nothing blew up while you were gone."

She scoffed. "Things blew up."

The fox shrugged. "Nothing important. Things blowing up is simply life in a big city."

"It's sad that I mostly agree with you."

A dozen unconscious or dead mercenaries lay scattered around a smoking crater in the center of the narrow, steep street. Abandoned houses with boarded-up windows stood on either side. Several of the buildings were half-collapsed, never repaired after an unfortunate showdown between a dwarf bounty hunter and a few bounties using poison magic a few months prior. Although the contamination had been contained to a small area, no one trusted the government enough to move into a place they believed might be both poisoned and cursed.

Somehow, when Dad blows something up, people become interested in it. How does that work?

Despite the property crash, the city still hoped for recovery, as proven by the well-maintained road. It had been in great shape before she blasted magic into it.

She sighed. Even if the city officials cut her a little slack for damaging the street, they would ask for compensation. It was a simple fact that insurance companies had long since become wise to the questionable return of investing in a Brownstone operation. Large payouts of any kind would cut into the profit margin on the job, especially since her PDA subcontract missions were always lower paying. Yes, she had the satisfaction of knowing that she provided a service to the country, but she didn't want to have to pay for the privilege if possible.

Mason jogged over to her and wiped the blood off his face. "Are you okay, A?" He stared at her shoulder. "Huh. Your shadow healing has improved. I can't even tell you were shot aside from the damage to your clothes and the bloodstains."

It had been some time since he'd seen her seriously injured, so his reaction didn't surprise her. Although she'd taken time off from work after the nonsense at the resort, that didn't mean she'd not practiced some of her Drow shadow magic techniques. The more skills she mastered, the more effectively she could end trouble without having to destroy city streets.

"Of course. It's not like I've spent all my time with Miar and Rasila playing mini-golf." She took a deep breath and tapped her receiver. At least it hadn't been destroyed in the battle. "How are things going with your team, Drysi? Were you attacked at all?"

"No," the witch replied through the device, her voice strong and clear. "Jerry's totally bored, and the witness looks a little scared. That's partially my fault, though."

"Why?"

The woman laughed. "I keep saying random things in Welsh using a really serious tone and then telling him, 'Don't worry about it. I have it covered.'"

Hana giggled.

Alison groaned. "Don't do that, Drysi."

"But I need to have a little damned fun. Your trick worked and I'm bored here. It doesn't matter, anyway. We're almost at the drop-off point."

Her boss didn't press the issue. Drysi had come a long way from the ruthless assassin for the dark wizards she'd once been. Teasing someone was far down on the hierarchy of sins.

Hana looked around and her eyes gleamed with playful curiosity. "Are we done here, then?"

"Not yet. We should hold our position until the cops get here, at least."

Alison looked at the armored SUV parked on the curb behind her. The dark-tinted windows blocked a view of the inside, and as far as the mercenaries had known, the witness they had been paid to assassinate remained in the vehicle.

Scratches and dents scored the paintwork, along with a few bullet holes. The blackened front and remaining scraps of the front left tire clearly indicated that the mercenaries had put in a good effort. If the vehicle hadn't been armored, their initial attack would have shredded anyone unprotected inside. Even with the hardened protective layer, the sustained enemy fusillade had made it through. Fortunately, the Brownstone team members inside were all prepared for an assault and the mercenaries didn't seem inclined to waste anti-magic rounds on a non-magic vehicle.

A smoking line of other vehicles stretched down the street, either bullet-riddled or burning. Alison didn't see the need to harden vehicles that had been empty.

It was supposed to have been a straightforward job. Her team needed to pick up a witness and transport them to PDA custody as part of a major push against a cartel that trafficked in artifacts. Unfortunately, the man was distrustful of portals and planes and demanded that someone drive his ass from Santa Fe to San Francisco. Based on intelligence received, the security team had formulated a distraction strategy that relied on several remote-controlled vehicles operated by Tahir and Sonya to fake a major convoy. Drysi provided direct backup to Jerry and his team in case the enemy didn't take the bait.

She stared thoughtfully at a dead mercenary who still clutched his rifle. They'd fallen for the trick, but a dozen men with rifles, even with anti-magic bullets, didn't seem like enough given the cartel's resources. She'd fought street gangs with more men. Had she been wrong?

"Tahir, do you see anything suspicious around Drysi and Jerry?"

"Nothing," he responded, his voice free of tension. "If someone's hiding near you or Jerry and Drysi, they're doing a very good job." A hint of offense crept into his tone.

Alison scrutinized the area suspiciously. "Considering the price on this guy's head, I'm surprised we didn't get tougher mercs."

Hana squared her shoulders and tilted her chin with a smug smile. "I think you forget how awesome we all are." She pumped a fist. "Can I get a Team Brownstone?"

Her two companions stared blankly at her.

She harrumphed and folded her arms. "You're boring now that you're married."

"I've always been boring compared to you," Alison pointed out. "And since when have we done a Team Brownstone cheer?"

The fox shook a finger. "It's never too late to start."

Mason grinned. "I'm comfortable with how boring I am and with how boring my wife is."

"I hope her brother is more exciting than her."

Alison smiled warmly when she thought about her baby

brother. "I think decades of concentrated Brownstone exposure will turn him into a barbecue-loving freak with a penchant for weapons. He might be many things, but boring? I doubt it."

"Things are about to become far less boring," Tahir interrupted. "A dropship with an unregistered flight plan is flying fast and low and from the south. The city has noticed them, but I've informed the local police that they are going toward you. They were already sending units to set up a cordon to deal with your aftermath, and they seem more than willing to let Brownstone Security handle the situation. They will destroy the dropship if it doesn't stick around."

"Blow them out of the sky, Alison," Hana suggested. "Before the cops take all the credit."

She shook her head. "Unless I vaporize the entire plane, who knows where it'll crash? If the local cops want to handle that part, let them. We'll take care of their packages."

"Some people merely need to know when to give up." The fox groaned and tapped her ring to infuse her skin with a red glow again. She drew her sword and a moment later, her tails winked into existence. Her eyes turned from brown to yellow with slitted pupils. "This is why I hate these kinds of jobs. There's no opportunity for me to charm anyone at all. Kicking ass is fun but sometimes, I want a little more subtlety."

"People don't hire Brownstone Security for subtlety." The Drow layered new shields over herself before channeling magic to her hand. A shadow blade coalesced into existence.

A dull roar that might have been easy to dismiss among the distant background noise of a major city unless they were listening for it grew louder. The black dot that appeared in the distance marked the approach of the drop-ship—a pretentious name, perhaps, for a glorified VTOL airplane.

Alison crouched in readiness and shadow wings spread from her back. "Come on, get it over with, assholes."

The seconds ticked by as the black dot assumed first the outline, then the solid, distinctive shape of the craft. It roared overhead with the back already open. Four men in scarlet power armor deployed from the aperture. Their heavy rotary machine guns came to life in the same instant and rained bullets on the SUV.

They still think the witness is in there.

She elevated rapidly and on a direct trajectory toward one of the falling armored assailants. The mercenary turned his weapon on her. She didn't dodge and his stream of bullets struck her shields and stung but didn't penetrate. It might have been a gamble on her part to remain in his line of fire, but no one would waste expensive anti-magic rounds by using them in a weapon that hungry. If the cartel was rich enough to afford that, they would have sent a team of wizard hitmen from the beginning.

Bullet after bullet struck the vehicle, sparked, or left cracks in the windshield. The constant barrage of high-velocity large-caliber rounds was too much even for the armored SUV. Cracks spiderwebbed and soon, slugs pierced through and drilled holes in the windshield. The body of the vehicle fared better, but that didn't stop the assault from reaching the inside.

They don't know it's empty, but that's now another thing I'll have to replace.

Two of the other mercenaries opened fire on her teammates. Both sprinted in separate directions and changed course abruptly every few yards to throw the enemy off. Apparently, they were more careful than she was. Given their relative power levels, that was a good thing.

Mason maintained his pace but raised his wand to deliver a fireball at the man who had targeted him. The spell didn't do much against the heat-resistant armor, but the distracted mercenary stopped firing briefly.

Oh, wait. What if they snuck the occasional anti-magic round in there?

Alison didn't have time to think deeply about her gamble. She closed in on the mercenary and slashed with her blade to slice deep into his armor. He didn't have an anti-magic deflector, but he didn't wear balsa wood, either.

A rune-covered blade emerged from his right wrist. She circled and stabbed into his neck. In an instant, he began to fall rather than fly.

She yanked her weapon free. The other power-armored figures fired breaking thrusters, but the dead man plummeted between his comrades to land with an echoing thud.

Hana flanked the enemy closest to her, a smile on her face. He pivoted and released a torrent of lead in an attempt to find target on the quickly moving nine-tailed fox. She came within range and stabbed with her enchanted blade. The blow dug deeply and her opponent stopped firing. She tugged the bloodied *tachi* loose and the merc fell.

Alison dived toward the man attacking Mason and Hana sprinted to him as well. The life wizard didn't bother with another offensive and instead, concentrated on a rapid serpentine sprint to avoid the stream of bullets. The two women reached the attacker at the same time.

The fox's quick chop cut the mercenary's gun in half. He threw a punch and a rune blade emerged but she dodged with ease and simply snickered. The Drow swooped overhead and sliced into his shoulder. The man jerked toward her, his face hidden under the helmet but his focus on her unmistakable.

The mercenary shouldn't have taken his attention off Hana but she made the most of his distraction and hacked aggressively through the armor. The *tachi* was one of the few human weapons Alison had ever heard of seriously injuring her father. It was arguably even more powerful than her summoned shadow blade. The lightning-fast blows penetrated with ease and stabbed him through the chest.

"I told you we were awesome," the fox crowed.

Something loud boomed in the distance.

"Now what?" Alison took a deep breath and landed. "Are there any other surprises, Tahir? Power armor was more than I expected."

"No," he replied. "The police shot the drop ship out of the sky after he refused to land."

"Oh, that's what that noise was."

Hana laughed. "See? Awesome." She offered the last part in a sing-song voice.

Alison chuckled. "Drysi?"

"We're at the drop-off point," the witch reported. "The PDA and FBI are here."

"Good. Then we're done and this is officially no longer our problem."

I'd rather hang out with Mason, but I guess it's good to get back to work.

CHAPTER TWO

Agent Latherby managed something approaching a smile from behind his desk. "I want to thank you, Miss Bro…" He frowned. "Is it still Miss Brownstone or Mrs Lind, now?"

"I'll keep Brownstone as my last name." She laughed. "It makes sense. There's too much professional recognition wrapped up in that name to set it aside—two generations worth. I'd have to change my company name and get new business cards. It'd be really tiresome. You know, you could simply call me Alison. That'll make it less awkward."

"Uh, Alison," he said a little reluctantly and with some discomfort on his face. "Your nuptials aside, I do want to stress how helpful your participation in this operation was. So much so that I've been authorized to give you a bonus. It's my understanding that the city government of San Francisco is presenting you with a rather hefty bill for some of the collateral damage."

She shrugged. "It's a hazard of the job."

"We'll cover that bill."

"Really?" She smiled. "Thanks."

"The witness testimony will help us and our law enforcement partners down south gut the cartel. It's only been a day, and we already have defectors running to the US and Mexican governments. They understand what's coming. Criminal cowardice is always helpful to facilitate the end of this kind of operation."

"That's good news. I'm always happy to be of service in taking down scumbags."

Agent Latherby stared at her with his eyes narrowed but didn't say anything.

Okay, that's not creepy or anything.

Alison coughed. "Is there something on my face?"

"I was thinking about how your skin is darker than when we first met. It's a subtle change, but it's there. I don't see you all that often, so perhaps it's more noticeable to me when I do."

She shrugged. "I'm half-Drow and my Drow magic has been getting stronger. It's part of the package."

He leaned back and nodded slowly. "You're not only a Drow, though. You're the Princess of the Shadow Forged."

"Yes, and?"

Where is he going with this?

"From your perspective, what's the situation with the Drow succession?" he asked.

"Why do you ask?" She frowned.

"The US government is aware that you've been in contact with other Drow princesses," he explained, his voice devoid of emotion. "Regular contact in some cases. They're also well-aware that at least one of those princesses has an assumed identity she uses for regular business on Earth."

"Huh, they've been more thorough than I thought." Alison kept her voice calm. "But last time I checked, none of them are wanted criminals on Earth or Oriceran. Of course, they probably don't file the appropriate paperwork for all the trips from one to the other, but if you followed up on every Oriceran who arrived for a day visit on Earth, it'd be a mess. That aside, how do you even enforce that down in the kemanas?"

Agent Latherby took a deep breath. "Yes, the Drow princesses aren't criminals, but they also aren't the kind of women who can be ignored. What is more, your contact with them has raised a few eyebrows among some in the government."

"What? The CIA's backing the Guardians, and they don't like that I hang out with people they consider counter-revolutionary or something?"

"Nothing even as carefully considered as that." The PDA agent shook his head. "It's not an exaggeration to note that we're still at a major disadvantage, both as a country and a planet when it comes to reliable non-open source Oriceran intelligence. All those centuries of covering things up mean the Oricerans get to be here in huge numbers, complete with semi-autonomous zones and a deep knowledge of Earth culture, and we still rely mostly on Oriceran ambassadors and consuls to clue us in.

"Even most Earth-born magicals seem to reflexively keep Oriceran business to themselves and idiotic policies kept open magicals limited to the PDA until recently. That has seriously gutted the ability of the FBI, CIA, and others to deal with magical matters. It'll take years, if not decades, to bring our magical intelligence community to where it needs to be in the modern world. As a result, it means we're not well-suited to evaluating political struggles over there, especially in an insular community like the Drow. But I want to make it clear that even if they had the capacity, there's no secret government plan to influence the Drow succession."

"You're telling me the government doesn't care who takes control of the Drow?" Alison scoffed. "I don't care if they're understaffed. There's no way they don't care."

"I didn't say they didn't care, but the US government is officially neutral in this matter." Some of the tension left Agent Latherby's face. "Even King Oriceran is doing his best to keep a hands-off approach. No one on either planet wants the Drow to believe they can interfere with any country on Earth with impunity. That's our primary concern."

She snorted. "Sure. They merely need to go to the Light Elves and the government and get them to screw with people's adoptions."

"Things are very different these days, Alison. Many people understand that mistakes were made."

"Do you ever think about that phrase?"

He furrowed his brow in confusion. "What phrase?"

Alison raised her fingers to make air quotes. "Mistakes were made." She shook her head. "It sounds so passive. It's like someone simply wandered around minding their own business and they ran into a big heaping pile of mistakes. But mistakes weren't made. People made mistakes, and those mistakes could have cost my dad his life at Laena's hand."

"Your father is one of the most pow—"

She slapped her hand on his desk.

Agent Latherby raised an eyebrow but didn't say anything.

"My father's tough, yeah. We both know how tough and how much everyone on this damned planet owes him, but that doesn't mean he's immortal. I like you, Latherby. You've never screwed me, and we've dealt with a number of criminals together, but I also know that not everyone in the government—let alone all the different Oriceran governments—have my best interests at heart or that of my family."

"Is there a point to this rant, Alison?"

She sighed, leaned back, and folded her arms. "I want that clear, especially since we're talking about the Drow succession. I don't want to have to watch my back because a senator or Light Elf consul gets it in his head that I'll be a problem and targets my family or me. You know we won't sit around and do nothing, and if anyone even glances at my brother, my father will destroy them and anyone on their Christmas card list."

"Fair enough and understood," he replied in a conciliatory tone. "What is your current official stance on the matter? We know you're in regular contact with two different princesses who, to the best of our knowledge, have different succession positions."

"I'm trying to be neutral in all this." She sighed. "Even though they keep trying to drag me into it."

"It's important to note that your involvement might be

inevitable. Even if the Drow lack the numbers to win a war against the United States, they could still prove a major problem."

Alison blinked. "What? A war?"

"There have already been several instances of pro-Laena terrorism."

"I've heard that."

"It's been controlled politically by the Guardians' firm denouncement and punishment of any Drow affiliated with that type of activity. That's one of the few reasons King Oriceran's reluctant to intervene, despite a recent incident of Drow terrorism outside their territory."

"Damn it." She gritted her teeth. "They need to get this crap settled."

"Exactly." Agent Latherby pointed at the ground.

She looked down, confused by the gesture. "Uh, nice carpet?"

"You've been to the Seattle kemana. You've seen what a group of dedicated fanatics can do. Even your recent vacation was plagued by similar issues. The Drow are natural shapeshifters and can be ruthless. What if they engineered a terrorist incident in a kemana that could be explained away as the work of dark wizards? Or perhaps they do something more subtle." He scowled. "Laena has sworn vengeance against not only the Brownstones but the United States. Terrorism can escalate into war. What would happen if a magical destroyed the White House, for instance?"

"Laena's a prisoner and stripped of her power." Alison swallowed, appalled at the thought of what he had mentioned. "Even if she wants to play a long game of misdirection, she can't."

"And she has supporters among the princesses. I know you understand much of this already, but I was asked to pass along some of the concerns of the US government. For now, and officially, they're neutral. Unofficially, the administration prefers if the Guardians maintain control, and they're—" His mouth twitched, and he averted his eyes.

"What?"

"I apologize, Alison, but they've made it clear they don't consider you becoming queen an optimal situation. Your father has his supporters in the government, but many people remain afraid of him and what he represents. The same could be said of you."

"It's best if I don't become queen?" She laughed. "That's something I agree with them on. Like I told you, I've tried to keep out of this but the Drow constantly appear and mess with me. I've leaned into at least establishing a relationship with some of the princesses who aren't total psycho Laena-lovers. The government might not want any of them to become queen, but I think we can all agree we don't want Laena back."

Agent Latherby nodded. "Indeed. We're doing our best to monitor things, but it's not like the old days. In this modern, magic-rich world, we can't track everyone who opens a portal. The Drow princesses can come and go with impunity, and we have every reason to believe our Oriceran contacts downplay trouble, despite reporting terrorism, and we have almost no real direct intelligence collection capability in Drow territory. So let me ask you this one question. I'm not asking you to betray any confidences or alliances you've made with any of those women. I only need to know what you feel the timetable of succession might be."

I could tell him to screw off. It's not technically their business, but he's right. If the wrong woman ends up queen, things will get messy, and too much of that mess will involve me. It might help if the government's on my side instead of trying to extradite me as a sacrifice to placate the new Queen Laena or Drae and avoid war.

"Based on what I've been told, I suspect a big move will happen soon, probably in the next month or two."

The agent nodded slowly and discomfort edged onto his face. "That soon?"

"Yes. Princess Drae made me offers that lead me to believe that. I think she wants to make her move and wanted me out of the way while she consolidated her power. I won't say that Rasila or Miar care about anything but the Drow, but if they become queen, I can assure you that they won't mess with Earth. Novati is dangerous and what little I've heard suggests she's pro-Laena."

"I thank you for your candor, Alison. If what you say is true, you'll need to be as careful as we will."

Alison uttered a grim chuckle. "Oh, trust me, I know. I want this to be over one way or another as much as you do."

"And you honestly have no intention to seek the throne?" he asked with a hint of suspicion.

"I have a company to run. I can't rule an entire people."

CHAPTER THREE

"I look like a damned flasher," Tyrone muttered under his breath. The weight of his briefcase tugged at his right hand and refocused him. His bulletproof trench coat might not be as stylish as he would have preferred, but the piece of clothing had saved his life on more than one occasion. He told himself he didn't believe in good luck charms, but it didn't hurt to have a few in his line of work. Being an underworld courier meant he often found himself in dangerous situations.

Normally, he didn't make his courier drop-offs in upscale residential neighborhoods. Something about the cookie-cutter houses with their identical lawns set him on edge. The drop-off location wasn't his choice, and his average client preferred to meet someone in the city far away from houses and the suspicious eyes of busybody neighbors. But his payment on this particular contract was too high to ignore or to argue.

It's not my problem if someone calls the cops on them. After I make the drop-off, I'll be out of this city for a few months. This is why I hate dealing with damned amateurs.

He glanced at his unassuming gray sedan. No one fired a gun or missile at his car and that was always a good sign. In his experience, many people liked to assassinate couriers immediately after they exited their vehicles. His next checkpoint was coming up as killing someone on the porch was almost as popular—although a street killing would at least save them cleaning.

Tyrone walked up the narrow crushed-granite walkway. The carefully manicured lawn on both sides screamed suburbs. He hated places like this. Everything about the pleasant flowers near the porch to the unoffensive color scheme hung over him like architectural oppression.

Everyone always misunderstood high-density urban living. He might have an apartment sharing a wall with someone else, but his neighbors understood how to mind their own damned business, exactly as he did. Out in the suburbs, you weren't up next to someone but they also wanted to be in your business and they cared about things like if you painted your house the right color.

They were the kind of people who would wonder why strange visitors might arrive at your house in the middle of the night or why a man in a suspicious trench coat headed to your front door a little past noon.

I'll never live in a place like this. I need to get back to NYC as soon as possible.

He jogged up the short stairs to the elaborately carved front door and didn't bother to knock. His instructions were to directly enter the house. He slid his right hand into a pocket and grasped his pistol as he prepared himself for another checkpoint. Holding his breath, the courier opened the door and stepped inside.

A plain-looking man in a suit stood calmly and inclined his head toward the door. "Please close that. I've taken appropriate precautions against spies but they won't work if someone can see us. Not only that, I'd rather get this over with as soon as possible. No offense."

Tyrone shook his head. "Give me the passphrase first."

"Is that really necessary?"

He lifted the briefcase. "It is if you want this."

"I'd rather be a king in hell than a servant in heaven," the man stated irritably.

The courier snickered and closed the door behind him. "Then you should never rely on a nickel defense."

"We've exchanged our foolish passphrases." The man gestured impatiently. "Please give me the briefcase."

Stupid overeager amateurs.

"You know how this goes," Tyrone replied. "I need to see my payment first. I get paid, and then you get the good-ies. I'll even throw in the briefcase."

There was no reason to bring back an item that a magical might be able to trace later. He'd learned that lesson the hard way a couple of years prior.

The suited man made a quick motion with his hand and murmured and a small figurine appeared on the table. It resembled a rainbow-colored anteater.

Tyrone frowned and his stomach knotted. "No one said anything about you being a wizard. That includes you."

"You didn't ask." The man smiled. "Perhaps you should be more careful next time if you don't want to be surprised."

Wait. If he's a wizard, how did he pull that shit off without his wand?

His heart rate kicked up. He kept his attention on the other man while he strode to the table to grab the figurine. It was warm to the touch and despite his discomfort, he grinned and tucked it into his pocket.

A Gabralin original. Damn, that gnome knew how to make a nice figurine.

Disdain flickered across the man's face. "You do realize that has no significant magic power? On Oriceran, they are nothing more than rare toys. Yes, they do change color depending on temperature and the mood of the viewer, but it's a curiosity. You can accomplish the same thing with modest magic."

"I collect them," Tyrone explained. "I'm only five away from a complete set. Unless Gabralin comes back to life, there will never be another like them." He set the briefcase on the table and stepped toward the door. "And what do you care? It's still expensive and hard to find."

"I suppose that's true." His contact gestured with his hand again and the door locked. "I hope it brought you some minor joy."

He sighed. "Come on, man. Don't do this. You have what you need in that little briefcase, and I have what I need—a toy, you said so yourself. Why would you complicate that by trying something stupid? We had a good thing going."

I should have known some shit was up when he made me come out to the burbs.

"You're a loose end," the magical explained. "To be clear, I bear you no special enmity, but it's very important that the item in that briefcase is used successfully and if you happen to mention it, that might complicate things. It's important for the future."

"The future of what?"

The man's form shimmered for a moment. A beautiful dark-skinned woman with stark white hair and pointed ears replaced him. Her suit was replaced by a low-cut purple gown.

A Drow? What the fuck?

"The future of my people," the Drow woman stated. She scrutinized him closely, her lips pressed together in disapproval. "You humans don't understand true leadership, especially the people of this land, but your delivery today will help to ensure that my people remain strong. There will be sacrifices, but they will usher in powerful leadership. They will grant the Drow a clear future destiny, one that has been denied them since Laena was deposed."

Tyrone rolled his eyes. "This is why I hate dealing with Oricerans. Look, babe, I don't give two shits about Oriceran politics or whatever moldy grudges you have over Legolas dissing Gimli two thousand years ago. I don't give two shits about my own country's politics. I don't vote, and I don't care who runs things. Shit, it's not even like I obey all the laws." He brandished his pistol. "And see this?"

"A gun. How quaint."

"I might have been a little surprised at your magic before, but I still came prepared. So, yeah, it's only a gun, but it has effective anti-magic bullets in the magazine." He yanked the belt on his coat and tugged the garment open fully. With a grin, he pointed to the anti-magic deflector hanging from his neck, the crystal completely clear. "And I made this investment a while back. Every once in a while, a magical thinks they'll screw me out of a payment simply because I'm a non-magical human and they're a powerful witch, wizard, or Ori. Sorry, babe. I hate to hurt someone as hot as you, so if you want to not be a bitch about this, you can unlock the door. I'll be on my way and you can use that little fun artifact inside that briefcase to do whatever you want. You can start a Drow civil war for all I care."

"I intend to murder a large number of people," she explained calmly. "Not without purpose, but there will be no mercy. I do this to end a Drow civil war before it starts."

Why are the hot ones always psychos?

"I already told you I don't give a shit about that political crap." Tyrone groaned. "I don't like trouble. If I kill you, I might get Alison Brownstone on my ass."

The Drow woman raised a delicate eyebrow. "Alison Brownstone?"

"Yeah, she's some Drow royalty and shit, right? That's why they call her the Dark Princess." He shrugged. "You don't see many Drow on this side of the gates, which makes me worry about her. So, let's end this, babe."

A faint chuckle built to mocking laughter from his opponent.

"What's so fucking funny?" he demanded. "I'm the one with the gun."

She raised her right hand and strands of shadows appeared from nothing. They twisted together into layers that formed into a long, thin sword of pure darkness.

"Don't do anything stupid, bitch," Tyrone warned. "I'm not above killing people. Don't think I haven't before."

The Drow smiled at him. "If you somehow managed to kill me, Alison Brownstone would praise you as a hero. I had some thought of letting you go. I considered you might be useful to provide her with misinformation, but after what you've said, I don't think I can let you go."

"Please." He patted his deflector. "I can empty my gun into you before you can get through this. Even Alison Brownstone can't cut right through one of these and she's a Drow princess."

The woman's nostrils flared. "She's not a Drow princess. She's a human pretending to be a Drow. She's a disgrace to the Drow people."

"Whatever. Fuck off."

"You've made a mistake," she murmured. "Your anti-magic deflector won't save you from normal weapons." All the emotion had left her voice.

"All I see is a spell blade." He scoffed. "Screw this. I gave you your chance." He fired twice.

The bullets passed through the Drow and she disappeared.

"Huh." He grinned. "I didn't think it'd be that easy."

"You're ill-prepared," his adversary whispered into his ear. "And far too willing to believe your eyes."

With a hissed intake of breath, he spun to face her where she stood behind him with a gun pointed at his head.

Tyrone swallowed. He dropped his gun and raised his hands. "We can work something out. I can do you a freebie."

"Because you're ill-prepared," she continued, "you're also sloppy and won't hide your tracks well. Thank you for your package. You've begun the process of restoring the rightful government of the Drow."

"Please, no, you don't—"

She pulled the trigger three times.

The courier collapsed and his collectible fell from his pocket and landed in the spreading pool of his blood.

CHAPTER FOUR

Alison popped the tuna *maki* into her mouth and savored the texture and flavor counterpoints that made Maneki sushi perfect and unique. Even the fresh sushi she had on vacation didn't compare despite being twice as expensive.

I missed Seattle more than I thought.

Reasonable pricing didn't mean much when her best friend seemed intent on eating her entire body weight in fish and rice. Even for a compact woman like Hana, that was considerable sushi. She had already finished a couple of mixed trays and few stray grains of rice clung to her full cheeks as she chewed.

"You're different," the fox insisted between mouthfuls. "I'm not sure if it's because you're married or you finally had a decent vacation."

"I'm not different. I'm the same as I've always been," she protested.

Hana shook a finger. "Trust me. I have a nose for this. You're still Alison, and you overthink everything, but you don't…" She scrunched her brow and stuck the tip of her tongue out of the corner of her mouth. "You're less tense. Or maybe it was all the honeymoon sex." She waggled her brows.

"Maybe. Mason has impressive stamina even without magic." Alison laughed. "I'm still surprised that no one is mad about my quickie wedding."

"We all simply want you to be happy." Hana picked her cup of tea up to take a sip. "And we've all wanted you to take time off for a while, but it wasn't like everyone expected you to have as ridiculous a wedding as your parents did, even though I think Ava would have been in her element planning that."

"I guess so. It's a strange feeling, though." A pleasant warmth filled her, and she'd not had any *sake*. "I know we were living together already, but everything feels more real and clearer now that we're married. The future has come into focus."

Her friend nodded slowly and set her cup down. "Uh-huh. But there is one thing I wonder about."

"No," she declared firmly. "Don't bother to ask."

"No? I didn't even ask a question."

Alison shook her head. "I didn't need to hear the question. You want to know if we're considering kids. Yes, we are, but not right now. We're both still in field-heavy positions, and that's not something that's compatible with raising a child. I can't worry about a little one when I'm still blowing holes in roads. Even my parents finally had safe jobs before they had a kid."

Hana snickered. "Your dad fought an entire Oriceran

war factory not all that long ago. I don't know if I'd call that safe."

"Yeah, but that wasn't part of his day-to-day routine. He normally simply does barbecue."

"Safe barbecue stuff. Like what happened in Colorado?" The fox giggled with the glee of a child getting her favorite present at Christmas.

She rolled her eyes. "Yeah, yeah, very funny. The point is that my current lifestyle isn't compatible with children or pregnancy, and that's before you consider I'm still deep in this Drow succession crap. The government's up my ass about it now, too, and it's only a matter of time before Drae sends a squadron of dragons to burn Seattle down to get me out of the running."

"Oh, there's the old pre-wedding Alison coming out," Hana chided. "But let's not worry about the Drow." She selected some salmon sashimi and swallowed it after a few careful chews. "You know, now that you're married, it makes a girl think."

"Has Tahir mentioned it?"

"Not much." Hana grinned. "Maybe I should flip it and ask him. It'd blow his mind. He wouldn't know what to do."

Alison tried to picture the kind of wedding Hana might have. It would probably violate several laws and treaties.

"And you're ready for that?" she asked with a faint smile.

The other woman sighed happily. "I do love him—annoying, boring parts and all. I think it's one of those balance deals. He's nice to look at, and I know he comes off stiff to everyone else, but I also know he really cares about me. I've never felt as comfortable with a man as I do with him. He doesn't care about my past or anything else. And Omni likes him."

Alison's phone rang. She couldn't ignore the custom ring tone, the "James Bond Theme" that identified the caller as Ava. Her assistant wouldn't bother her at dinner without a good reason.

"What's up?" she answered.

"I apologize for interrupting your meal, Miss Brownstone," the woman replied. "Under normal circumstances, if a client barged in and demanded to see you immediately, I would have sent them away and rebuked them for their impertinence."

She sighed. "It's not your fault. So, who is it? Let me guess. A Drow?"

Hana set her latest piece of sushi down and muttered something under her breath while she rolled her eyes.

"If only," Ava replied. "No. It's a gnome who identifies himself as Mr D. I thought, given your history, that you would be interested in meeting him sooner rather than later."

Alison burst out laughing.

"Is it really that funny?" Ava asked.

"Yeah, it is. Circle of life. If it wasn't for his job, I might not ever have come to Seattle. That means I might never have met Hana, Mason, you, or so many other people."

"Never met me!" Hana threw her hands up. "Oh no. Alternative timeline dystopia Seattle." She clutched her shoulders and shuddered. "I wonder if I'm a dreary Goth chick in the alternate timeline."

She chuckled. "I'll be right there, Ava."

Mr D remained standing while Alison took her seat behind her desk. He wore a crisp tuxedo and a bland, unassuming smile on his face as if he knew all her secrets.

I still don't know much about this guy, but at least the job he had me do before made the world a better place.

"Thank you again for coming to talk to me on such short notice, Mrs Lind," he began. His vowel emphasis was off, exactly like it had been when she'd last talked to him. That was a small concern compared to his choice of address. He hadn't actually used a name or title during their brief conversation before heading to her office.

"I still go by Brownstone," she clarified. "It'd be too inconvenient with the business cards and that kind of thing."

"Very well." Mr D didn't speak for a few seconds. Instead, he surveyed the room with a curious glint in his eyes. "I'll be efficient. Your time and my time are both too valuable to waste. I wish to hire you for a very unusual and dangerous job. Since you're now free of the unfortunate affliction you possessed when I initially hired you, I suspect you'll find this job easy, if not trivial."

Alison frowned. "You actually said it was unusual and dangerous."

"Inherently, yes, because of the nature of the job, which is why I've come to you. I've followed your career. Your power has continued to increase, and the catalog of foes you've defeated grows impressive—perhaps, some might even say, legendary." The gnome folded his arms behind his back. "I came to you because I was confident you would be able to handle this job. It's as simple as that. This is a personal matter, so I wish to ensure success."

That sounds matter of fact, but he might be buttering me up.

"Okay. What's the job?"

"I need you to recover something for me. Unfortunately, I've become aware that ill-mannered people are also seeking it."

"Recovery?" Alison was impressed by how still the gnome stood. "That sounds familiar. And what am I recovering? Another dangerous super-gem? A jar full of imaginary genies who like to rap?"

Mr D's mouth quirked into a wry smile. "If only it were so simple." He took a deep breath and shook his head, his expression disappointed. "I had a nephew who ran into trouble several centuries ago on Earth when he helped some humans with a little political experiment. I won't go into all the details as they are fairly irrelevant so long after the initial events, but he earned the ire of certain magical factions, including some rather unpleasant wizards. At the time, the only way he could evade his pursuers was to go into a type of protective suspended animation and send out a message to his family requesting assistance."

Alison nodded slowly. "Okay, this all makes sense so far, but it sounds like something went wrong."

He inclined his head. "Indeed. He was attacked in the middle of his final spell and so, among other things, the beacon spell that was supposed to lead us to him despite his wards wasn't properly enabled." He clucked his tongue. "We therefore had no idea where he was. In addition, the backup part of the spell—which was supposed to ensure he came out of suspended animation in a few years—wasn't successfully cast. The theory was that even if the beacon failed, he'd be able to set up a new one."

"And so it lasted a few centuries? It's finally shut off, and he's sent out an SOS?"

The gnome shook his head. "No. As it currently stands, the suspended animation will effectively last forever." He tilted his head. "I suppose it becomes irrelevant once your sun expands and consumes the planet, but even gnomes don't live for billions of years, magic or not." He reached into his jacket and pulled out a small purple candle, crossed to the desk, and set it in front of Alison. "This will serve as a beacon for me, regardless of where you are. It can best most wards. Simply light the candle with any form of magic near him, and I'll be able to use other artifacts to recover him."

She frowned. "If you don't even know where he is, how am I supposed to find him?"

"I came into possession of another artifact recently that enabled me to find him when supplemented with the help of a few dragons and a powerful ritual," Mr D explained with a bored shrug. "Those specific details are irrelevant. The important thing is his location, which I was able to ascertain is in the southern Gobi Desert. He's in a subterranean tomb complex. There aren't any major population centers around it."

"I'm a security consultant, not a tomb raider."

Then again, I know a few tomb raiders.

"This is a recovery job, exactly like the first one I hired you for. It merely involves an unusual location and a person instead of an item. I don't see that it's at all different. I even saw on the news that you recently assisted with moving a witness. It's all the same idea in principle, and I wouldn't ask for your aid if I thought you wouldn't be able to successfully execute the job, which is, as I've highlighted, a personal matter."

"That makes sense," Alison conceded. "And if there's no one around, that at least means I don't need to hold back as much, but you said at the beginning that this would be dangerous. Is it because of tomb guardians or that kind of thing?"

The gnome shook his head. "If it were that simple, I would handle this matter myself. The people my nephew ran afoul of were a particularly nasty faction of dark wizards, a sect that has operated in Russia since ancient times known as the Shadows of Rurik. Unfortunately, while they don't know the exact location of the tomb complex, my sources tell me they are very close to finding it. They're not only interested in particular artifacts from the tomb, but they have a long-standing desire to punish my nephew for disrupting some of their plots in the past. I won't claim that everything he was involved in was acceptable by human standards, but I can assure you those wizards are objectionable by everyone's standards."

She frowned at him in confusion. "Are you telling me they're pissed about something that happened hundreds of years ago?"

"Of course. One doesn't need to be a gnome to harbor a long grudge. If anything, being shorter-lived means they have to carry such burdens with greater intensity to better pass them to the next generation." Mr D shrugged and looked more amused than concerned. "I hope that even though they aren't affiliated with the Seventh Order, your involvement in this matter might frighten them off. Your extreme methods of dealing with dark wizards have become well-known in the greater magical community."

"They started it, but you're saying you don't want a fight if you don't need it?"

Mr D nodded. "I'm interested in recovering my nephew, not wiping out a faction of dark magicals. I'll leave everyone else in the world to handle that. I'll make this as easy as possible for you and will even portal you directly to the site. I need your muscle, as it were, Miss Brownstone, not your brain."

"But it's still effectively a tomb raid," she said thoughtfully.

"Will that be a problem? I'm surprised to see you so hesitant."

"I'm powerful, but that doesn't make me all-powerful." Alison grinned. "And it won't be a problem. It merely gives me an excuse to bring in a friend who specializes in that kind of thing. Before I agree, I'll need to clear it with my team and I'll need a few more details."

He spread his hands expansively in front of him. "Whatever you need that's relevant, I'll provide."

"Let me call my assistant in to take notes and we can get started."

CHAPTER FIVE

The Brownstone team gathered around the conference room table. Not only were Ava, Mason, Hana and Drysi present, but Lily was as well. Even though it'd only been a day since Alison talked to Mr D, the Gray Elf tomb raider had rushed to Seattle to help her friend and make a little extra money on the side. No one objected to the idea of taking on the job, although they decided to limit it to Alison's team. Supporting an entire contingent of non-magicals in the heart of the Gobi Desert wasn't practical.

"I merely want to get this out of the way," Alison began, "but no one has any objections to Lily coming along, right?"

Mason shrugged. "We've all seen what she can do."

Hana gave a thumbs-up. "If we have to raid a tomb to steal a body, who better than a tomb raider to help us with it?"

"It's not a body." Drysi snickered. "The little bastard's still alive…kind of." She frowned. "What if he isn't alive?"

Alison sighed. "Then we deliver his body to Mr D so he can give him a proper funeral. But he doesn't strike me as someone who'd send us all the way out there if he didn't have good reason to believe his nephew was still alive."

I feel like someone else mentioned a gnome needing his nephew rescued. Is there something where gnome nephews get in trouble often? Or maybe that was a cousin. I can't quite remember.

Ava remained quiet and tapped notes to cover the meeting. She'd already dug up a pile of background research and provided it for her boss to look through prior to the briefing.

Alison put her fist to her mouth and coughed. "Okay, then, like I told you yesterday, we have the coordinates and we have confirmed it's in the Gobi Desert in southern Mongolia. There should be no risk of collateral damage to people. We're supposed to not destroy the tomb if possible, but Mr D has said he'll handle all the political wrangling in terms of damage."

Lily's gray eyes twinkled with amusement. "You mostly don't want to start setting off explosions when you're underground to avoid cave-ins."

"That, too."

Drysi pumped her fist in the air. "Fucking perfect. I won't lie to you, Alison, sometimes it's nice to be able to cut loose and not worry about if a spell will blow up a school."

Alison eyed the Welsh witch. She didn't even want to know when she had come close to blowing a school up.

"We might not need to go that crazy," she cautioned. "Mr D's handling a slew of background paperwork to make this all nice and legal. He has various political contacts, and the Mongolian government apparently owes him a few favors. Like I said, if this all goes badly, he'll take the blame, not us, but I still want to avoid screwing him over if possible."

"The client taking the hit?" Hana rubbed her hands together. "That's a nice change of pace. We'll be two for two for that kind of thing this month."

Alison shook her head. "Remember, this won't be us simply walking in there and pulling the gnome out. We have guaranteed magical traps and hostile magic creatures, and that's assuming the Shadows of Rurik don't show up and want a piece of him."

Hana frowned. "Who are these guys exactly? What's their deal other than having a beef with Mr D's nephew?"

She inclined her head toward Ava. "She dug up as much background information as she could, and it all confirms what Mr D told me yesterday. That said, there aren't many of them. The Shadows have allegedly been around since before there even was a Russia and have pulled strings for as long. It's not confirmed, but many people believe Rasputin might have been a member."

"No wonder the bastard was so hard to kill," Drysi muttered.

"Even after the opening of the gates, they remain mysterious," Alison explained. "And the Russian government actually has them listed as an illegal magical terrorist organization and have tried to eliminate them for at least ten years. This isn't only a Russian matter, though. The US government recognizes the validity of the bounty even within US borders."

Mason's brow raised. "If they're so mysterious, why does the Russian government care so much about them?"

Alison shrugged. "The official story is they have interfered with Russian history in a negative way, but there's not very much detail. There is, however, a level five dead-or-alive organizational bounty on the entire group put out by the Russian government. Mr D's worried that they're both interested in killing his nephew and also potentially snatching artifacts from the tomb."

Lily sighed. "I'm a tomb raider, so I think about things differently, but are we so sure these guys are that bad?"

"I don't know," the Drow admitted. "But Ava's research didn't find anyone who had anything good to say about them. They might have even been involved with several nuclear accidents during Soviet days." She shrugged. "But they're not our target. We're supposed to rescue Mr D's nephew. If the Shadows don't show up, we won't go looking for them. If they do, I'll give them their chance to surrender or leave us alone. If they choose not to, it's bonus time. Simple as that. I merely didn't want anyone surprised."

Hana tilted her head, a puzzled expression on her face. "By the way, what's the name of the guy we're supposed to save? You never mentioned it."

Alison laughed. "Mr D said he would answer to Kut but that wasn't his actual name. I didn't bother to press him on that. After all, he's a gnome who goes by Mr D."

"When do we go?" Mason asked. "If these Shadows are sniffing around, shouldn't we arm up and let him portal us over there ASAP?"

She shook her head. "He told me it'd take a few days to

finish the legal preparations with the Mongolian government. It turns out they're a little nervous about allowing the Dark Princess and her friends to go there."

Hana grinned. "It's not like we blow stuff up all the time."

"It's not a big deal. They do owe him a favor but he also doesn't want to cause an international incident. We'll get our gear ready today, though. There's no reason to not be prepared if luck goes our way."

Lily cracked her knuckles. Her long gray hair swayed as she glanced at the others around the table. "A whole elite team of magicals for a tomb raid. This will totally be fun. I'm used to working alone, but I don't mind serious backup."

"Again, keep in mind we're only there for the nephew," Alison insisted. "Part of the conditions of the Mongolian government letting us in officially is that we're not to take anything else out. They will arrange their own expedition to recover artifacts, magical or otherwise."

Hana snickered. "Translation, they want us to disable all the defenses and do all the hard work before they loot the place."

"Probably, but Mr D's paying us enough that it shouldn't be a problem. If all goes well, this will be a very profitable few days."

Alison jerked awake in bed and rubbed her eyes.

Wait. What? Why am I awake?

Mason sat up beside her and yawned. His outline was

barely visible, illuminated by the soft light of her phone. Her brain finally adjusted and she realized it was ringing.

"Who the hell is calling me in the middle of the night?" she grumbled and snatched up the device. Someday, she'd have a job where she could silence it at night without being concerned about missing an important call. With a sigh, she looked at it. The caller ID clarified the situation.

"I know there are time zone differences, Mr D, but it's the middle of the night," she said by way of greeting.

"I understand," the gnome replied, "but I wanted to inform you of what's going on because it will affect our actions going forward. There have been complications that require adjustments."

She rested her head on her soft pillow, her phone still to her ear. "Is the Mongolian government not playing ball?"

"No. They are quite receptive to my suggestions. It's a lack of preparation on my part. I have not visited the location directly. I simply located it and I underestimated the power and complexity of the remaining wards. There is unusual magical resistance over the site, and we won't be able to portal there unless you're willing to risk the portal collapsing and death."

"I'd prefer not to die. Or at least to die later than sooner."

Mason looked at her with a raised eyebrow. It was a typical response to another half-overheard conversation as the husband of Alison Brownstone.

"I can understand that desire," Mr D assured her. "The new plan isn't particularly complex. You'll need to fly using conventional means. I'd suggest a supersonic flight. Even if you were allowed to bring all the necessary weapons onto the magic train, there are no Starbucks in Mongolia."

"A little plane ride doesn't bother me." Alison yawned. She didn't need clients waking her up in the middle of the night. "But it's not like we can take that plane directly to a hidden ruin in the middle of the desert."

"No, that's not practical. You'll fly to Ulaanbaatar. I've arranged for a VTOL transport to take you the rest of the way to the site. That should account for any strange magical resistance. I won't accompany you to the site, but you can still use the candle as a magical beacon once you've located Kut. I'll also provide a satellite phone with various enchantments. They might not function properly within the barriers, but it's still an impressive and expensive phone with normal technological functions."

She moved her legs to the side and set them on the floor so she could sit on the edge of the bed. "A little plane ride isn't the worst thing I've had to deal with on a job."

The gnome uttered a quiet chuckle. "No, I'm sure it's not, but there are more complications beyond that."

"Of course there are." She snorted. "Lay it on me."

"The site is completely subterranean. It's sealed, but I'll provide you with a small artifact gem that will open it. It will also lead you to it."

"What's with you and magic gems?"

"It's not a terrible interest to have," Mr D replied, his tone sharp. "What you should be concerned about is that my Mongolian contacts have made it clear the tomb is in a magical no-go zone."

"No-go zone?" Alison stood. The job was dangerous

enough, but at least it was straightforward. Last-minute problems were annoying.

Mason shook his head, a faint smirk on his face. He only needed to hear her side of the conversation to know how complicated things had become.

At least someone's not worried.

"Yes," the gnome continued. "The area has an unusually high level of magic relative to most places on Earth, but there's no known kemana there. The accompanying presence of an equally unusually high level of magical monsters might be responsible for lack of said kemana. It's always had a cursed reputation, but once the gates began opening, it became, in the words of one of my contacts, a part of the desert known to swallow man and beast."

"If it's that dangerous, why hasn't the Mongolian government cleaned it up? That sounds like stuff they put in a tourist brochure to scare people."

"The monsters naturally cluster only in a single, large area, and they've made no effort to expand beyond that. I'm sure there's some deep mystery there, but they would prefer not to risk destabilizing the situation and potentially risk directing monsters toward more populated areas in Mongolia and surrounding countries."

Alison took a deep breath and slowly exhaled. The universe was leveling things out after the easy witness escort job.

"So, it'll be a pain to travel to the site, and it's probably crawling with monsters on the outside and inside. Is that everything?"

"That's an accurate summary," Mr D admitted. "I'm sure it's nothing you can't handle."

"Wait." She narrowed her eyes. "If they're so worried about disruption, why are they letting someone like me go into the area?"

"To be clear, the magical area doesn't center on the tomb complex. It simply happens to be in the vicinity. They are comfortable with a small team being inserted into the locale, and they feel you'll do less to potentially agitate the situation than the Shadows of Rurik if they can find and access the tomb." A faint wisp of amusement entered his voice. "Not only that, I'm sure the rather generous donation I made to their national archaeological preservation fund was helpful." His tone returned to serious as if his humor had never been. "I understand the increased risk. While I will increase your pay, I'm willing to let you back out. I didn't provide sufficient initial background when I hired you, and I'd rather have a pleasant relationship with you than sour it by forcing you into something you don't feel adequately prepared for."

Alison looked at Mason, who rested on his side, his elbow bracing him as he watched her. "I'm fine with it. I'll double-check with my team, but as long as no other surprises appear I don't think there will be a problem. Does that work for you?"

"Fine. We'll speak again in your morning." The gnome ended the call.

She groaned as she put the cell phone on the bedside cabinet. "I'm really missing our honeymoon."

CHAPTER SIX

Drae stood in the center of a forest clearing surrounded by towering fir trees. A few curious birds sat on the branches and tilted their heads from one side to the other as they watched the two-legged intruder.

She had shape-shifted into a light-skinned Wood Elf—a fitting disguise, given the setting. The form only needed to last for an hour. Her next tool would arrive soon, and once she passed along what she'd discovered, her true plan would begin.

A more direct strategy might have been helpful, but this will work and my patience will be rewarded. Laena's greatest mistake wasn't her attempt to snatch Alison Brownstone. It was in not sending her warriors to kill the girl when they had the chance.

The Drow princess half-closed her eyes and a soft smile spread over her face as she thought about the death of Alison Brownstone. The false Drow had grown quickly in power over the years—far more quickly than any of them had ever anticipated. That alone was enough to justify her death, even if it wasn't necessary to save the Drow.

They were dying. The Guardians denied that, but Drae, Princess of the Deepest Night, understood it. Laena was flawed, but she'd provided unity and direction. Now, with the weak Guardians in control, the fear of the Drow faded. Their enemies became bolder, both on Earth and Oriceran.

It would be a major concern under normal circumstances, but not all the other princesses understood the threat. Miar and Rasila let themselves be polluted by Alison Brownstone. The former even supported the Guardians. Novati lacked the necessary cunning to become queen. Drae was the only one who could save her people and provide them the direction and leadership necessary to bring back the true strength of their people.

But too many were watching the Drow. Too many were watching her. Subtlety would be required, along with sacrifices for the greater good.

The weak perish to nourish the strong. Such is the way of existence. All the Drow princesses should understand that. If they don't, they will perish to nourish me.

She'd already collected one necessary artifact from the disgusting human courier she'd killed but now, she had a chance to strike a blow at one of her greatest enemies without it ever being linked to her.

Magic rippled behind her. She turned as a beautiful witch with crystal-blue eyes and short blonde hair appeared in the clearing. The new arrival's dark hooded cloak concealed most of her body, but her wand hung from her slender fingers. It was Drae's contact, Tionna Solokova.

There was something about her eyes that the Drow liked. They were so cold and ruthless. The woman would be an excellent tool.

Drae raised a hand in greeting. "Welcome," she said in Russian. "It's a pleasure to meet you."

Tionna sneered. "I don't care about pleasantries, elf," she replied, also in Russian. "I'm here because you went out of your way to get my attention in a way that might end with your death."

She nodded. "I wanted to meet you because I have something useful for you. I came across information you might find interesting, and I'm willing to give it to you."

"So your message said." The witch tightened her grasp on her wand. "You are bold to contact the Shadows of Rurik. I should kill you right now. You know who we are, which means you're a risk to us. Tell me why I shouldn't kill you and I'll consider it."

Arrogant little witch. If only you knew who I was.

"My death doesn't benefit your cause." Drae gave her a cold smile. "But I have no problems with your group. To be honest, the intricacies of Earth magicals aren't something I care to spend time learning, and I can't bring myself to care about which groups do what on Earth. Do the Shadows intend to invade Oriceran? Then, and only then, will we be enemies."

"What if I told you we intend to kill innocent people?"

"Innocence is a relative thing. Deaths on this planet aren't my concern."

Tionna watched the Drow with narrowed eyes, her mouth pressed into a thin line. "Then Oriceran is not our concern. We have no desire to interfere with matters there."

"Very well, then. I'm not your enemy. Besides, you'll

want the information I have." Drae spread her hands in a friendly gesture.

"Nothing comes without a price," the woman muttered. "What do you want? Money? An artifact?"

The Drow princess shook her head. "Nothing so vulgar. I want you to kill someone for me."

Tionna snorted. "The Shadows aren't assassins for outsiders. Don't think you can tempt me so easily."

She smiled. "I can assure you that once I share this information you'll want to kill this woman anyway." She raised a hand.

The Russian's arm snapped up and she pointed the wand at Drae's face. "My desire to not be your rabid pet doesn't mean I find violence objectionable, elf."

"I simply intend to show you something you'll find interesting," the Drow explained in a calm voice. In other circumstances, she would have killed the insolent witch but the tool would be cast aside only after it served its intended purpose.

"Slowly," Tionna insisted. "Or you die."

Drae murmured her spell and made a few intricate motions with her hand. A full-sized image of a smiling woman appeared between the witch and Drae, a Gray Elf.

I've watched you, Alison. I know all about your little friend Lily, and I know she's with you now.

"Her." Tionna lowered her wand. Her eyes widened as she crept toward the image. "Do you have family, elf?"

"Yes," Drae replied. "They are loyal to me, and I to them."

"I had a sister once," Tionna murmured. "We weren't

close, and we'd parted because of her refusal to join the Shadows, but she was still my blood—my kin." She stopped. "She disappeared abruptly, but I investigated more than I should have and even gathered powerful artifacts to help my search." Her mouth curled into a hateful sneer. She pointed at the image of Lily. "The life of the apprentice will be adequate compensation for the death of my sister Yulia."

Excellent. All my efforts in investigation were not wasted. Perhaps if your mother hadn't become sloppier in recent years, Alison, I wouldn't have learned about many of the people she's killed in the past. It makes it easy to manipulate all those around her, including you.

"Then we're in agreement," Drae declared. "This tomb raider has vexed me in the past." She summoned another image, this time a globe. It spun in place until Mongolia appeared and zoomed in on the Gobi Desert. "I've learned she will raid a tomb complex somewhere in the Gobi Desert. I don't know what she's seeking there and I don't know the exact location of the complex, but I have taken measures to discover when she arrives in the country, and I will pass that along to you."

Tionna stared at the map in disbelief. "A tomb in the Gobi? This could be the lost tomb of the Great Khan. Some believe it's the burial place of Genghis Khan himself. Others believe it's another ruler, but all agree it is a place of great magical power."

"Is it now?" Drae shrugged. "I was less concerned about where she was going than who was going."

She'd come across some of that in her research, but her

apathy was genuine. Her efforts on Earth were to support her power and the Drow alone. If she could slam the gates shut, she would. For now, she needed Tionna and her associates to strike at Alison, and dangling Lily as bait would force them to do so.

Admitting from the beginning that Alison Brownstone would be involved might frighten the witch off. Although Drae had little confidence that Tionna and her allies in the Shadows of Rurik would be able to kill her, if they slew even a single one of her allies, the false princess would suffer and become easier to defeat later.

Even a small advantage will increase my chance of victory.

"You don't desire the power from the tomb?" Intense incredulity infused Tionna's voice. She kept her wand up, ready to cast at any suspicious movement.

"No. I didn't even know what it might be until you told me. Oriceran is my home, not Earth. This Lily needs to die because she has interfered with my plans. She has wronged you personally. We both get something out of you killing her. There is nothing deeper in it than that. You are many. I am one. You have a better chance of killing her."

The witch lowered her wand slowly before she slipped it under her robe. "She might not be alone. It won't be so trivial to kill her. She can see into the future."

Drae turned to leave. "I give you this information freely so that you might deal with a mutual problem. If you choose not to follow it up, that is your concern. You can decide what your sister's vengeance is worth."

"Contact me when she's in Mongolia," Tionna insisted. "And I'll handle it from there."

"Very well." The princess walked away smiling.

I don't care what fear and false prophecies have wrought. I will rule Oriceran but first, I need to ensure the proper Drow becomes queen.

CHAPTER SEVEN

Her sore butt found little relief, no matter how often Alison shifted. The cushions were allegedly some kind of fabric, but she wouldn't have been surprised if a mage had transmuted them all to metal. The seats bolted into the center of the transport plane's cargo hold totally lacked comfort.

Two rows of five narrow seats were positioned near the back of the cargo hold. Alison, Mason, Hana, Lily, and Drysi all filled the front row.

"I preferred the first-class seats on our way to Mongolia," Alison complained. "I flew all the way from Seattle and felt comfortable, and I'm on this thing for less than an hour, and it's like the Seventh Order has gone to war on my butt."

Mason snickered. "You can't always travel in style. The honeymoon spoiled you, I think. You're soft, Alison."

"I simply don't want my ass to be sore before I've even gotten in a fight."

Hana laughed.

Alison rolled her eyes. "You know what I mean."

The fox looked up and to her left, a smirk on her face. "Sure, whatever you say."

Drysi snored, her head lolled to the side and drool oozed out of her mouth. It was only an hour's flight, but the witch had complained of jet lag and that magic hadn't helped much. Alison suspected some last-minute drinking might have been involved, but the witch only needed to be awake when they were on site.

Her attention drifted to the pile of crates strapped in netting along the walls of the hold. They were filled with guns, gadgets, and drones. If everything went well, they would be in and out of the tomb within a day, and one way to ensure that was to bring the appropriate gear. Mr D couldn't provide specific details on the threats.

Dad would probably say there's no such thing as overkill.

The plane shook when it encountered a pocket of turbulence but no one displayed any concern. That was another thing that separated Alison from her father. There was a certain irony in the strongest man on the planet being afraid of flying. Even if he fell out of a plane, as long as he had his amulet, he wouldn't die. At this point, she wasn't certain he'd die if he fell from the border of space.

Hana ran her hand along her thighs. "Alison's right. These seats suck. We should get a bonus for this part."

Drysi murmured something in Welsh. She blinked her eyes a few times before she opened them fully. "Are we there yet?" She looked around the cargo hold. "We're not dead. That's a good start."

"We're almost there," Alison replied. "About five to ten

more minutes. We'll disembark and they'll take off and come back if Mr D can't resolve the ward situation."

"Why don't you disable them?" Hana asked.

"It's not that easy. We're talking centuries-old wards cast by a gnome and who knows who else. It could take me a long time to find a way to disable them."

Drysi sighed. "It had to be a damned desert, not a beautiful tropical island."

Alison was tempted to mention the island of Nereids, but beyond the fact that it wasn't strictly tropical, it might also be a sore point of conversation given why Drysi had originally accompanied Brownstone Security there. Sometimes, she forgot that the Welsh witch was originally an assassin for the Seventh Order.

"It's a job, not a vacation," she mumbled. "If you want time off, get married and have a honeymoon."

The woman threw her head back and barked out a laugh. "I don't think there's a man ready for me yet."

"It's better than Antarctica," Lily suggested. "I've been there more times than I like. It's not that fun. Penguins are cool, but everything else sucks."

Alison gestured to a square black case holding a drone. "At least Tahir will be able to help us. All Mr D's information only indicated a problem with magical wards, not signal disruption. He can still control the drones even with that. And you're still okay with us using him, Lily?"

She thought about calling the infomancer but decided against it. They could all gear up with their receivers once they were on the ground. It wasn't like there was a key piece of information he would need in the next few minutes.

Lily's relaxed smile was infectious. "I don't normally go on tomb raids with an entire team, so I'm fine relying on your resources. This will be the easiest job I've had in a while."

Hana turned her head slowly toward the Gray Elf and a hungry grin appeared on her face. "Alison's taken the plunge. What about you? You make her parents' engagement look short by comparison."

The elf groaned. "I don't know. It'll happen when there's a good time. I'm not in a hurry. Harry's not in a hurry. You go first."

"Maybe I'll do that. Don't tempt me." The fox laced her fingers and stretched them above her head. "I think this job will be fun as long as there aren't any nasty bugs in there."

"There could be." Lily grinned. "You never know what you'll find in a place like this. It's been sealed off for hundreds of years, right? It could be overrun with the most disgusting giant magical bugs you have ever seen. And this area has much higher background magic, so we could encounter some hardcore magical monsters."

Hana's gaze dropped to the long sheath lying in her lap, no doubt imagining all the giant bugs she would need to slice in half. "I should have known better than to agree to go on a tomb raid with Lily. This will be that roach nightmare all over again."

Drysi snickered. "The little bastards die easily enough."

The fox grimaced. "You weren't there. They weren't that little. Do you know how many showers I had to take before I felt clean?"

The plane shook again. It dropped a few feet and Alison's stomach lurched with it.

Turbulence isn't a big deal. That's what they always say. I wish my stomach agreed.

Lily took a deep breath. Her pupils dilated for a moment. She jerked forward with a gasp a moment later. "We're about to be ambushed. They need to land the plane right now."

Oh, shit.

Alison didn't question her friend. There were advantages of bringing someone along on a job who could see into the future, even if the ability was limited. She ripped her seatbelt off and layered a shield before she sprinted toward the front of the cargo hold.

The others removed their seatbelts and Mason and Drysi cast shields spells. Hana foxed out and activated her ring, replacing the young attractive woman with the vulpine-eyed, clawed nine-tailed monster with a red sheen. She finished by strapping her sword belt on.

"I don't even have a wedding planned yet," she muttered.

The turbulence made crossing to the door connecting the cargo hold to the cockpit more complicated than Alison expected. She slapped her palm on the intercom call button. "You need to get the plane on the ground now. We're about to be attacked."

The pilot scoffed. "No offense, Brownstone, but leave the flying to us. We have nothing on the radar. If you're saying we don't have a landing zone, can't you go clear that for us before we come down?"

She peered through the window. The copilot frowned and stared at the radar, gestured to it, and looked forward.

Come on, Mr D. You had to hire people who wouldn't take me seriously?

"Listen to me," she shouted. "Lily's half-Gray Elf. Do you understand what that means? We need to—"

A pulse of magic surged quickly before the blow struck. A massive explosive consumed the front of the cockpit. To her surprise, the reinforced cargo hold door held, but the sudden drop of what was left of the craft launched her to career through the cargo hold. The lights died and plunged the interior into darkness. Her back stung from the collision with the roof but her shield took the brunt of the hit. Red emergency lights flickered and gave an eerie cast to the thick smoke outside the door.

A few seconds passed before Alison realized she hadn't fallen. Another few seconds passed before she understood the reason was that the rapid descent of the back of the plane pinned her to the roof.

And some people pay to experience this kind of thing.

She managed to turn her head. Hana clung to her seat, her claws sunk deep into the top. Mason and Drysi remained standing, a slight glow around their legs. Both kept a tight hold on their wands.

Alison's stomach lurched as the plane continued its free-fall toward the desert below. The roar of the air rushing past was deafening. Smoke choked the nose of the plane, but a slight shift revealed there was nothing left. Whoever had attacked them had annihilated the front in one blast.

Damn it. The pilots didn't even have a chance.

Without a clear view of the ground, she had no idea how long they had until they made impact. They had been flying low, to begin with. At least they still had wings—that might to help with some feeble stability, although it was debatable how effective they would be.

Alison layered another shield over herself. If they had more time to plan, maybe they could have saved the plane. Her heart thundered as she watched her friends. They were all protected, but would it be enough? It wasn't every day they were in a plane crash.

The entire aircraft rattled as it continued to plummet. Metal buckled and glass shattered as the body of the decapitated plane met the ground. The initial collision sheared a wing off and ripped the hold open. Bright light from the unrelenting sun pushed back the dim red interior glow.

She bounced around the interior of the plane like a pinball and felt each blow with some discomfort, but her shields protected her organs and bones. In the chaos, she tried to look for Mason and the others, but the constant motion combined with the glass, metal fragments, and loose packing cases made it impossible to confirm anything. A hint of a glow in the corner of her eye one moment was rapidly replaced by a tumbling witch in the next.

The continued momentum sheared away more pieces of the aircraft to create several jagged tears and leave their smoking, broken remnants scattered in a rough line on the light-colored sand. An abrupt jerk ejected Alison through one of the gaping holes in the cargo hold. She arced and gritted her teeth as she summoned shadow wings to arrest her unexpected flight.

What little remained of the body of the transport plane

bulldozed for a few hundred more feet, smoking and on fire. The other wing lay a hundred feet behind her in several pieces. Smoke poured from the burning wreckage and floated into the cloudless sky.

Yeah. That was fun.

Alison took several deep breaths as she surveyed the area. Judging by the dark smoke and light glinting off metal, pieces of the plane had spread over miles. No one had their receivers in at the time of the crash. They hadn't expected to be shot out of the sky.

They're okay. They have to be. They work for me and wouldn't let a little something like a plane crash hurt them.

A glowing red flare blazed skyward a few hundred yards away. It exploded in a shower of red-orange sparks.

She flew toward it, holding her breath. Mason's khaki-clad form came into view, his wand pointed straight up, and she exhaled a sigh of relief. She approached close enough that she could wave to him. He shook his wand in response.

Another flare streaked upward nearby. She pointed to it before she nodded to him and moved in that direction, keeping low to the ground. There was no reason to give the enemy any easy shots.

Drysi sat on the ground with a few cuts on her face but otherwise, in good shape for someone who had been in a plane that had virtually been demolished. Alison didn't stop moving until she was ten yards away.

"Mason's over there." She pointed in his direction. "You walk that way while I look for Lily and Hana."

"Fucking wonderful start," the Welshwoman grumbled and tucked her wand into a belt holster. She squinted at the sky. "I didn't think we'd actually have to walk in this shit." She tugged her jacket on.

While Mason had worn a khaki shirt and cargo pants with heavy boots, Drysi wore her leather jacket and jeans. It wasn't all that bad for a tomb raid, but she'd need to use magic to counteract the desert heat.

The local area defined desolate. Huge sand dunes dominated the scene all the way to the horizon with not even the faintest trace of vegetation. Columns of dark smoke drifted skyward and at least provided something to break the monotony.

Alison ascended, her heart rate slower than before but her stomach still clenched with apprehension. Mason and Drysi could cast direct protective spells, but Lily and Hana had only their artifacts and reflexes to save them. Would they be enough?

She drifted higher and scanned the landscape below in all directions for some sign of her friends. The heat haze made it more difficult to discern individuals, but a shimmering glow that moved erratically caught her attention. She altered course toward it until it resolved into a nine-tailed fox in a sprint with all tails on display.

Hana's near-blur speed slowed to a jog. "It's hot out here," she complained.

"It's the desert."

"Yes. Deserts suck. This is why I live in Seattle."

Lines of dried blood smeared the side of Hana's face and her forehead. The red gleam from her ring was gone, and the bronze artifact defensive pendant lay around her neck but it wasn't glowing.

I didn't even realize she'd brought that along. Good thinking, Hana.

She pointed to the pendant. "Did you have that on during the crash?"

Her friend shook her head and raised her hand. "Only the ring, but it's out of juice for a while. I had this stuffed in my pockets. All praise the cargo pants."

Fortunately, she'd chosen a reasonable outfit, including khaki cargo pants. Alison was half-convinced before they set out that Hana would demand to wear tight shorts and a pink sports bra on the mission with a matching feather boa based on some of her initial complaints.

Another flare blazed skyward. This time, when the sparks separated, they formed words.

LILY IS OKAY AND HEADING TOWARD US.

Alison breathed a sigh of relief. She felt bad for the pilots, but there was nothing she could for them but avenge their deaths.

It wasn't a random monster that blew us out of the sky. The Shadows of Rurik must be close.

CHAPTER EIGHT

The reunited team stood under the shade of a small dune transmuted into a dark, thin open tent. The spell wouldn't last long, but it was enough for comfort, especially for Lily and Hana who couldn't easily cast spells to counteract the heat. They didn't want to strain themselves for comfort. A whole tomb full of traps and monsters was waiting.

Lily could see into the future, but she had to be careful. Too much use of her ability meant she could get stuck looking at the wrong time.

They'd taken a few minutes to heal their injuries. Everyone's artifact and shields had held, and other than Hana not being able to use her ring, they were still in good condition for future battles. Their crates and cases lay destroyed, the contents scattered over the desert, but between magic and food bars tucked in pockets, they would survive for a day. Kut could still be rescued.

Alison needed to make sure everyone agreed with that plan first. She still had the candle and the gem. Even if Mr

D couldn't portal to them, he could bring another plane, but that presented its own difficulties. Being surprised one time was justifiable. If it happened the second time, it'd be incompetence.

"I've never run the company as a dictatorship," she began and looked at each of her friends. "And we took a big hit. Two men are dead. I don't know if they could have done something had they listened to me, but we're stranded in the middle of the desert." She retrieved the gem from her pocket. A smoky arrow inside pointed to the southeast. "Fortunately, we have a magical GPS that's still working despite the interference. We can still complete the job."

Hana wrinkled her nose. "It smells weird here. Magical but weird."

She nodded agreement to her friend's observation. A thickness permeated the air along with a lingering magical sensation that suffused the entire area. She'd noticed it once she'd no longer had to worry about her friends.

Mr D warned us, but now that we're here, it's everywhere. I didn't feel it up in the plane, though. Whatever they have set up here must not extend that high.

Lily dusted her hands on her pants. She'd lost a few pockets from her tactical vest in the crash, but she'd otherwise been unharmed. "In my vision, I saw some kind of rune-covered rocket. It was definitely magicals."

"It has to be those Rasputin assholes." Hana patted the hilt of her blade. "But they had their one shot, and we lived. So they'll die. They totally made this raid into a giant trap-and roach-infested tomb go well beyond annoying."

"Yeah, I doubt there are dragons spitting rockets

around here." Alison surveyed the area again. Despite the strange background sensation, there were no obvious magical spells and no monsters approached them. If it were the Shadows of Rurik, they might not have any ability to directly scry into the area from the outside. The team probably had time before their adversaries followed up their attack.

"I want to make sure that's what everybody wants," she continued. "We lost the satellite phone in the crash, but I'm sure Tahir's already poured through satellite imagery and verified that we survived. Knowing him, he won't call for another plane unless we do something to tell him."

"Like what?" Drysi asked.

"We carve, 'Tahir, send help,' into the desert, for example." Alison shrugged. "Or I can use Mr D's artifacts, but it'll be a big hit to our reputation. We still have a job to do, and we're here so I don't want to leave."

Mason grunted. "We didn't agree to die on the job for him."

"We're not dead yet." She licked her parched lips and unclipped a small canteen from her belt. There hadn't even been a need to fill it with magic yet. She took a sip. "We can track the tomb with the gem. We're almost there already."

Hana narrowed her eyes and peered at a dune in the distance. "Tombs are cold, right? At least it'll get us out of this heat."

Drysi looked at her jacket, regret written all over her face. "We were almost there in a plane, Alison. It might have been slower than the one we took to get to Mongolia, but it's not a fucking boat. It'll be a hike."

"I know. Doing the math in my head, we're probably

still twenty to forty miles away, but if you, Mason and I all use enhancement magic on Hana and Lily, we should be able to hike there without too many problems. It'll merely take a few hours." She shrugged. "And if we try to get Tahir's attention or use the candle, we might still be sitting here in a few hours."

Hana made a face. "We're hiking through the desert for a few hours?"

Mason's pinched expression made him look unusually disapproving. "Are you sure about this, A? Yes, we can do those kinds of spells and if we don't push it, we won't be exhausted, but we're already at a disadvantage from the crash."

She lifted the gem. "Exactly. If the Shadows of Rurik shot us down, they're close enough that they might find the tomb."

"They haven't attacked yet."

"Maybe they're on their way to the tomb. They might not even know we survived yet. If there are powerful arti-facts in there, I don't want them falling into the hands of twisted dark wizards. Not only that, even if we do call for a rescue, the next plane or helicopter will simply be shot down, too."

Hana folded her arms with a frown. "Tahir could call for military help."

Alison gestured toward the sky. "The Mongolian government is worried about trouble. The last thing they'll do is send military help into a dangerous magical no-go zone."

"Won't that be a problem no matter what we do?" Drysi

asked. "We'll eventually need help, and if that gnome can't open a portal, someone will be shot down."

"No, because if we're right, whoever shot us down is probably ready to follow us or on their way to the tomb. Once we deal with them, we can evacuate without trouble." She punched a fist into her palm. "Besides, we owe the pilots. We need to finish this job and eliminate whoever killed them."

Drysi shrugged. "We're already here, but next time, seriously, pick a damned tropical island."

"I have your back, A," Mason assured her.

Hana sighed. "I suppose they did try to blow us up."

Alison nodded. "Let's get the spells going and start our hike. We have a gnome to rescue."

CHAPTER NINE

Sonya bit on a stick of strawberry Pocky, chewed for a few seconds, and enjoyed the counter-play between the biscuit stick and the sweet coating.

I'm not simply a kid. I'm a witch and I'm an infomancer.

She sat at her workstation surrounded by screens lit up with windows that displayed everything imaginable, including feeds from drones a few blocks away to the individual temperatures in different rooms in the Brownstone building. Arcane runes flowed in one window, their colors pulsing in patterns she had memorized.

Magicals like her and Tahir would be the future, not stodgy people at magic schools shouting old-school incantations while they dropped the eye of newt in a cauldron. She respected Alison, but Sonya also suspected that she would have been fine if she had never attended the School of Necessary Magic.

Oriceran's strength was magic. Earth's strength was technology. It only made sense to mix them. The technomancer CEOs who screwed with Alison were criminals, but that didn't mean that technomancy and infomancy themselves were evil.

She slumped in her chair, the half-finished Pocky stick hanging loosely from her mouth. While she might be a witch and infomancer, she very much did not want to be at work at seven at night.

Without a doubt, she would have preferred to have been home studying for her drone battle race competition, especially with the upcoming Fall Classic. Recreation would have to wait, sadly.

With Alison and Hana out of town, she was staying at the Brownstone building. Tahir didn't mind her staying at his place, but he had also declared that Alison's absence would be a good time for them both to be extra vigilant. It was hard to say he was more paranoid than usual since his baseline level was already super-high.

He acts like a giant fireball-spitting werebadger will bust our door down any second now.

Sonya had been the same not all that long before. It was hard to live with the most powerful woman in Seattle and not end up less afraid of random surprise threats. He suggested that was the wrong attitude to have but his arguments hadn't been persuasive.

A little resentful, she finished the rest of her Pocky and yawned. She wanted to go home and do something fun, not sit there monitoring the drone, camera, and ward networks at night. The damned sun wasn't even up anymore.

This is so not fair. Why does Tahir get to watch Alison from home, but I have to stay here?

She shifted to try to find a more comfortable position.

It was frustrating and comforting at the same time because she knew the answer to her complaint. That was the problem.

It's safer here with Alison out of town, and they want to make sure I'm safe.

They kept her out of most of the major meetings, but she wasn't simply some stupid kid mascot. She provided active support both to Alison and Jerry's teams. She'd already gone through nasty betrayals, including her own father, not to mention her abusive mother. While she didn't mind being protected by the Dark Princess, she wished Alison, Tahir, and Hana would at least be honest about why they were worried.

Try and act like I can understand. Is it really that hard, man?

Sonya slapped her cheeks. She shouldn't feel sorry for herself. Then again, maybe she wouldn't if they didn't have her butt in a chair at work.

"Alison's more relaxed since coming back from her honeymoon, but she's more obsessed with that Drae chick," she mumbled. She'd overheard Hana mention the other Drow princess trying to make Alison agree to some kind of deal and how they worried that might mean an actual attack was imminent.

The whole situation was weird. Magic was one thing, but Oriceran princesses fighting for the throne? Sonya wasn't the kind of girl who had grown up wanting to be a princess and based on what she'd seen, there was only one reasonable conclusion—being a princess sucked.

She reached toward her half-empty, long, rectangular Pocky box that lay near the side of her keyboard. Her hand froze as an alarm window popped up in her central monitor.

BACKGROUND ACTIVITY DIFFERENTIALS BEYOND EXPECTED PARAMETERS IN COVERAGE SECTOR 24-A.

"This had better not be another stupid raccoon," she muttered. "I swear they're all transformed witches screwing with me." She snatched her mouse, accessed a drone feed drop-down, and selected the appropriate window before maneuvering a few other drones nearby so she would have cover from different angles. Tahir had drilled that recon technique into her head. Multiple angles meant multiple options, he always said.

The different angles didn't change what she saw—a narrow alley a block away from the building with a few sparse light bulbs to provide the dimmest of illumination. A light breeze blew a few stray wrappers down the narrow corridor. There wasn't a dumpster in sight but there were a few doors leading to businesses on either side. Nor was there a single raccoon in sight.

"The algos are programmed not to flag any of the normal employees of places around here. Did they hire someone new?" Sonya tapped her lips with the tip of her Pocky before she bit into the sweet snack. She should demand a snack bonus.

With a frown, she typed in a command and replayed the relevant drone feeds for the minute before the alert but merely saw more trash in the wind. Checking the wards would be pointless. They didn't extend off Brownstone property. Alison didn't want to piss off any of her business neighbors.

Sonya didn't get it. The idiots should be happy to have free Brownstone Security protection.

"Tahir's always telling me to think ahead. If I was a magical criminal, I might want to watch the building without tripping wards, but…" Sonya smirked. "I might be too stuck on magic and forget the power of tech." She clicked on one of the active drone feeds and changed to a thermal camera. "You can't hide from me, man. Don't you know who you're dealing with?"

The red-orange silhouette of a humanoid appeared in the center of the alley. Their head was tilted upward.

The young infomancer scoffed. "So you noticed a drone, huh? Too bad. I know you're there now. You shouldn't have been so cocky." She retrieved her headset from a drawer and turned it on with the flick of a switch. A quick click on her screen set her to the appropriate frequency. "Tahir, there's trouble."

He chuckled but a grimness underpinned the sound. "That's one way of putting it."

"Did you check the feeds?"

Tahir cleared his throat. "No, I was still monitoring Alison's flight. Their plane was shot down."

Sonya's breath caught. Her heart thundered and she barely noticed the invisible figure begin walking. Tahir had delivered the news so matter of factly, yet his boss and his girlfriend were on the plane.

"I… They can't be…" Her lip quivered and she tried to fight off the tears that threatened to escape.

"They're fine," he clarified. "I apologize for not explaining that upfront. I have clear satellite images of them. Yes, I had to borrow access to a few satellites, but if the government's people are good enough to realize I've done that, I'll handle it myself when they come for me. Our people survived the crash and are now continuing with the job. I've tried to raise them on their receivers and they're not working. I don't know if they don't have them, if they lost them in the crash, or there is simply excessive interference. There's a similar issue with the satellite phone."

"Shouldn't we send reinforcements?" She wiped a few tears from her eyes. Her heart maintained its gallop but now, at least, she knew everyone she cared about hadn't been killed. She was also more relieved than she expected that Tahir wasn't a total heartless asshole.

"If Alison needed that, she would have made it clear," he replied. "It's unfortunate that whoever was flying the plane didn't survive, but there's nothing we can do about it." He sounded a little frustrated. "And because of the distance involved, even if I borrowed a drone from the capital, it'd take too long to be useful. They know what they're doing, but I presume you didn't call me about that."

Sonya swallowed. She'd almost forgotten. Her suspicious invisible stranger hadn't escaped the drone network. He had stepped out of the alley but he hadn't moved closer to the Brownstone building, either.

"The drones tagged someone on thermals who is invisible on the camera scans," she explained. "Humanoid, roughly elf or human size, with normal body temperature. He's about a block away on the sidewalk and simply standing there like a creeper."

"I see. That is suspicious, but I wouldn't worry too much." Tahir almost sounded disappointed.

She frowned. "We have someone hiding himself with

magic only a block away from us. How is that crap not something to worry about? Come on, man."

"Because I'm doubtful that anyone would attack the building by themselves," he replied, his tone even and calm. "Even without our strongest people here, we have significant resources, and I suspect anyone who plans an attack won't be satisfied eliminating only a handful of people."

"I'm one of that handful of people, jerk," she responded huffily.

Tahir chuckled. "I've trained you too well for you to die so easily. I'd be very disappointed if you did."

If only she were on video chat so he could see her roll her eyes. "I'll keep that in mind. Do you have a plan other than depending on me being super-awesome and fighting off some super dark wizard assassin with the help of a couple of the early shift security and Sienna?"

The administrative assistant was working late to help Ava with a quarterly internal records review. Sonya didn't know all the details but had generated a few database queries based on Ava's requests.

"Yes," he assured her. "Although not entirely. As Alison's out of contact and halfway across the world, I'll contact Jerry. His team is on standby this week. We can rotate squads at the building until Alison returns and I'll come as well. If a wizard, a witch, and multiple squads armed with anti-magic bullets and deflectors can't repel the intruder, we can at least stall them long enough to request AET or PDA assistance. For now, set up active perimeter alarms." A few seconds ticked by before he spoke again. "And if you feel your life is in danger, let me point out it's more important that you preserve it for future improvement in your skills than to do something foolishly brave that will end with you dead. The line between bravery and stupidity is thin."

Sonya rolled her eyes even more dramatically than she had the previous time. "Sometimes I don't know what Hana sees in you. You could have simply said, 'Be careful, Sonya.'"

Tahir snorted. "If you understand my intended communication, why are you complaining? Save your derision for legitimate grievances."

"Whatever, man. I'll get to the perimeter alerts while you call Jerry. Should I contact security?"

"No, I'll contact them and let them know to be more alert. In truth, they're mostly there as tripwires against common criminals anyway."

The teenager smiled, all the tears and worry gone. Tahir could be a jerk, but he was an impressive infomancer. Jerry and his team might not be magicals, but with her help, they'd dealt with tons of dangerous enemies. If something did happen, it wouldn't be like when the Seventh Order attacked. This time, they knew it was coming. If someone planned to attack the Brownstone building, they would regret it.

Her fingers flew across the keyboard. "Bring it on, Mr Invisible."

CHAPTER TEN

Tionna dug her fingernails into her palm. The pain wasn't distracting. Instead, it was clarifying. Warm blood seeped from the self-inflicted wound.

She glared at the two wizards standing in front of her. Leonid and Adrian were both technically her superiors in the Shadows of Rurik, but while they had accomplished nothing in months, she had brought them a potential lead on the tomb of the Great Khan. All she had asked was one simple price, but her brethren had failed to deliver.

How can we accomplish what we need with such incompetence?

"They survived?" She hissed her fury, unclenched her hand, and wiped the blood on her robe.

A pile of femurs lay stacked in front of them with a skull on the top, the only significant feature of the sparse stone chamber. Flickering red candles surrounded the altar and the wax glowed at the base. Lines of scarlet light ran from the bottom of the candles in a jagged path to form a radiant net beneath the entire macabre assembly.

The combination artifact was one of the few powerful ones available to the Shadows, but if her information was correct, it might become a minor tool.

Leonid nodded gravely. "At least some did. We can't be sure from outside the area, but there are at least two other magicals who survived. Continued attempts to scry have failed and the telescope spell couldn't provide great detail, but we know they survived, at least, as they sent each other messages with flare spells. We've also confirmed that Alison Brownstone is likely with the Gray Elf. Given the people who are probably participating in her group, we believe the elf survived."

"They sent messages to each other?" Tionna narrowed her eyes. "That means whatever the magical interference of the area, it's not complete anti-magic. The rocket and their spells prove it. This changes things. It means we can handle this directly instead of relying on feeble attacks from outside the area."

Leonid frowned. "Did you not hear what I said? It's not only the Gray Elf. It's also Alison Brownstone. We've attacked her."

"Yes, and?"

"Don't you understand what we've done?" Disbelief flashed over his face. "We went along with this plan because of the chance to find the tomb. Killing this tomb raider was one thing. She was only indirectly related to the Brownstones but now, we've struck against Brownstone directly. You know what she did to the Seventh Order. We risk the annihilation of the Shadows with this attack."

"Are we such cowards now that we would hide because

of one woman?" shouted Tionna. "Alison Brownstone is merely one woman."

Adrian snorted. "Spare us, Tionna. This isn't about the Shadows. This is about revenge for your sister, a woman who turned her back on us. We only didn't target her ourselves because of her past service. And now we should risk destruction to avenge her?"

"Do you think this is only for Yulia?" She marched up to the wizard until their faces were mere inches apart, her expression locked in a mask of rage. "So what? Blood calls for blood, and it doesn't matter? If Brownstone and Lily are headed toward the tomb, they will have to be eliminated anyway if we want to take what's inside." She locked gazes with Adrian and dared him silently to disagree.

He backed away. "We can invade the tomb and take artifacts. We simply have to be quick about it. It might not be worth fighting Brownstone. If we avoid her attention, we won't deal with the risk of her retaliating against us. We could set up a distraction."

"Is this what we've been reduced to?" Tionna threw her hands up in disgust. "She's powerful, but she's not immortal. Besides, we don't have to defeat her to make it clear that she shouldn't dare to counterattack. I've already asked one of our brethren for assistance. I have another plan to humiliate and make it clear to Alison Brownstone that she dare not oppose the Shadows of Rurik. If we kill her in Mongolia, it'd be more efficient, but at least we have another option."

Everything about the attack was personal, but she honestly didn't care. It'd taken her years to learn Aletheia's true identity as Shay Carson-Brownstone. She'd considered vengeance before, but Shay was never far from her husband and challenging James Brownstone with anything short of nuclear weapons was suicidal. Striking at Shay's adopted daughter held appeal but would require aid. Now, as if by providence—infernal or divine—she had been handed an opportunity to kill both the apprentice and daughter of the woman most responsible for her sister's death. There was no way she could pass it up.

Tionna pulled her wand out of a robe pocket and held it in front of her, a vicious grin on her face. "By the time this is over, I promise you that not only will we have the treasures of the Great Khan, but we will also be the group that tamed Alison Brownstone."

Sonya hummed to herself as she strolled through a hallway with a Dr Pepper can in hand. It was annoying that she had to go all the way to the break room to get one, but Tahir complained about her using either magic or machines to get drinks. Passive exercise, he called it. She rolled her eyes at the thought.

I don't go out in the field. Why does he even care? I need this caffeine because I have to work a night shift.

It'd been a couple of hours since she'd seen the invisible stranger, and although she'd lost track of him when he ducked into a restaurant down the street, there had been no big attacks or any sign that other suspicious enemies were gathered in preparation for an attack.

"Maybe it was merely a wizard paparazzi," she mumbled. "Is that a thing now?"

Her eyes widened when the distinctive sense of magic pulsed through her. There was something familiar and powerful about the sensation, but it wasn't as if she could identify a spell merely from the texture of the magic.

Crap. Are they opening a portal directly into the building? Can they even do that?

She sprinted toward the source. The intensity of the spell made it easy to identify the general direction. She might not be a battlemage, but it made no sense to run all the way back to her workstation. Tahir was already there as well. He had to know what was going on and might be preparing countermeasures.

Should I head toward them, or is that dumb? I can at least stall them until one of the squads gets here to kick their butts.

The teenager picked up the pace. She turned hard right as she approached the lobby and a scream echoed from the room. Spells might be difficult to identify given the earlier magic, but the terror's source was easier. It was Sienna, one of the administrative assistants.

No, no, no. Where the heck is security?

A little out of breath and now seeing the wisdom of Tahir's concern over exercise, Sonya raced toward the lobby. She fumbled at her belt, but her fingers found nothing. To her horror, she realized she didn't have her wand. It was still inserted into her keyboard.

"Oh, crap." She swallowed a surge of apprehension. A witch without a wand might be okay if she at least had a potion, but Dr Pepper didn't count as a magical brew.

What am I going to do? Bite their ankles?

When she entered the lobby, she stopped and looked around in bewilderment. A new problem had replaced those she'd assumed she'd face. There weren't any intruders to explain either the magic or the scream.

Sienna knelt behind the front desk, her hands on her head and her eyes wide.

"Is he invisible?" Sonya demanded and her gaze scanned the area quickly. An invisible wizard wouldn't be ready to fight, and she had a chance to win using social engineering. She slid her hand to the top of a Pocky box in her back pocket. "Listen up, man. I might be young, but I'm a trained witch who works for Alison Brownstone. If you don't want me to bust you up and send you home crying about how some teenager kicked your butt, you'd better appear right now and put your arms up." She let her hand hover over the box. It was a little small for a normal wand, but an invisible magical raider might not judge the size accurately.

Tahir might be her mentor, but Hana had taught her a few things about how to trick people using nothing but a few words and gestures. All great hackers needed to be able to hack people as well as machines.

Give them a reason to believe. That's what the fox always said. *It's easy to trick people if you point them toward something they already expect.*

Heavy footfalls sounded from the hallway. Jerry's squad? Security? More enemies?

Sienna remained behind her desk and continued to whimper.

Sonya backed toward a wall but held her hand near her back pocket. She couldn't give the enemy any reason to believe she wasn't ready for a magical duel. "Sienna, are you okay?"

"I'm so not okay," the administrative assistant squeaked. "It'll eat me!"

"Huh? I don't see anyone. Who?"

"The monster."

The enemy might have used some kind of hallucination spell, but the young infomancer hadn't sensed anything else since the initial pulse of magic.

Jerry and four of his team rushed down the hallway, their assault rifles in hand and anti-magic deflectors hanging from their necks. They fanned out and raised their weapons, leaving nothing to chance. If a wizard suddenly appeared, he would receive an anti-magic round in his forehead.

"What's the situation?" the team leader demanded.

Sonya licked her lips. "I'm not sure. Sienna screamed, but I can't see anyone." She waved at a roof camera in the corner. Tahir had to be watching. "I'm not sure if they're invisible or if she's under the influence of mind magic."

Ava emerged around the corner a moment later with no gun in hand. Her pace was swift but her expression was as unperturbed as always. The teenager suspected Zeus could appear and rain lightning on the building and the woman would ask him if he wanted tea once he was done.

Sienna raised a trembling finger to point at the huge fish tank in the lobby. "Don't you see it? It'll jump out and eat me. I hate them so much."

They all turned toward the tank filled with colorful fish, including some that glowed. There was a pile of brown rocks on the bottom Sonya hadn't seen before, but she usually didn't pay that much attention to the fish so she couldn't be sure why it was different.

"What's the big—" she began.

Thin, dark, dumbbell-shaped slits appeared near the top of the rocks. After a few seconds, their shade of brown changed and blended less with the other pebbles and stones around it. Eyes became evident and it became clear that it wasn't a pile of rocks but a small octopus. The cephalopod floated up, its sucker-covered arms swaying gently in the water and its eyes looking directly ahead.

Sienna shuddered. "That thing is so creepy. It wasn't in there when I went to the bathroom, but when I came back, it was. Is it a kind of special Oriceran attack octopus?"

Sonya walked over to the tank, her head tilted as she stared at the unexpected addition. The octopus stared in return but made no hostile movements or seemed inclined to attack any of the fish swimming near or around it.

That's why that sensation felt so familiar.

"It might be an attack octopus, but it's our attack octopus." She laughed and gestured to the creature. "It's Omni."

"Correct," Tahir said over the intercom. "I checked the last few minutes of camera footage. Omni crawled into the tank in lizard form a few minutes ago. He burrowed under the pebbles where the cameras couldn't see him, and a few seconds later, the octopus emerged."

Jerry raised his rifle and flipped the safety on. "Damn it. I don't think anyone had octopus in this week's Omni pool. I didn't even think he could turn into one."

Ava strolled toward the tank, her hands clasped behind her back. "Given what we have seen him become, I doubt there's a single form on this planet he can't assume if he's so inclined."

Sienna sighed. "Oh, it's only Omni and not an Oricieran

attack octopus?" She shook her fist at the cephalopod. "I'm so telling Hana on you. You scared me."

"I would suggest we return to work for now." Ava cleared her throat. "The next unusual event might involve something other than Miss Sugimoto's pet."

CHAPTER ELEVEN

Trekking through the desert for a couple of hours might not have been part of the plan, but it also wasn't nearly as unbearable as they had anticipated. Once they began to walk, despite the bright sun, the temperatures were reasonable. If they hadn't had to begin their march directly after a plane crash, they might not have even felt as hot as they did. All the sand notwithstanding, it somehow lacked the painful scalding temperatures one might see in a place like the Sahara or even the Sonoran Desert. The endless dunes didn't make it all that pleasant, but it ultimately felt like an autumn hike in the world's most desolate area.

Ava had briefed them on what to expect, but it had slipped their mind in the original chaos. It was as if they saw sand and sun and their minds, combined with the desperate struggle to survive, convinced them it was hotter than it was.

This isn't fun, Alison thought. *But at least we're not under constant attack.*

In addition, her assistant had also warned them that the night temperatures would be chilly. With their tents and other gear destroyed, that might prove an issue, but given all the spellcasters present, they could manage.

No obvious ruins were visible in the distance but for the last ten minutes, the number of dunes had decreased and the arrow inside the gem grew more solid. They were definitely close and no one had spoken for a few minutes.

"I don't mean to be a downer," Drysi said finally, "but what do we do if the gem doesn't work? That gnome already underestimated a few things about the job, and I don't want to have to wander through the fucking desert for hundreds of miles looking for a tomb lost centuries ago."

Alison kicked at the sand. "In that case, we leave a message for Tahir and think of a way to communicate. If the plane wasn't in thousands of pieces, I'd suggest we try repair magic."

"Even if we could get enough of the aircraft, magic has its limits," the Welsh witch muttered. "And it's not like any of us know how to fly a plane." She finished the observation with something in her native language. Alison wasn't sure if it was a curse or not. Many of Drysi's Welsh statements sounded like she was angry or swearing about something.

Hana crouched low and drew her sword. Her eyes shrank to thin slits. "Do you sense any magic other than the weird background magic from before?"

Alison concentrated for a moment before she shook her head. She tucked the gem in a pocket, summoned a new shield, and infused strands of light and shadow magic into it. "Why?"

The fox turned slowly, her sword held high. "I smell something weird. It seems kind of familiar, but I can't place it—strong and sweet. It doesn't smell like magic to me, but it's not like I've traveled the world and sniffed every spell there is. It's become stronger over the last minute."

Drysi drew her wand from her holster and chanted a shield spell. Mason began his own defensive preparations.

Hana took a hand off her sword and placed it over the pendant. "*Corpus meum defendat. Custodiat animam meam.*" Faint light infused the accessory. "I wish my ring recharged faster. It's so much easier than this thing."

Alison held her arm out and concentrated magical energy into a shadow blade. "They might finally be coming after us. It could have taken them this long to realize we were still alive, or even to get here. It's not like they can portal in any more than we could."

"The Shadows of Rurik?" Mason asked.

Lily took a deep breath and looked off into the distance.

"What do you see?" Alison asked.

The Gray Elf's pupils dilated and her breathing grew shallow.

"Earth to tomb raider," Hana quipped and waved her *tachi*. "None of us can see the future."

There was no response from the elf.

Drysi grimaced. "Shit. She's stuck, isn't she? Does that mean we're fucked?"

Alison shook her head. "Not necessarily." She walked over to her friend and shook her shoulder with her free hand. "Hey, snap out of it."

The fox's tails burst into existence. Her claws extended from her hand and she growled. "The scent's growing stronger. It's everywhere."

Scratching sounded from all around them, followed by a light rumble.

Alison shook her friend. Lily fell forward, her eyes still open, but didn't react.

"Mason, I don't know what's about to happen, but can you protect her?" she asked. She inclined her head toward a dune in the distance. "If they target you, I'll make sure they focus on me."

Mason jogged over and scooped the lithe Gray Elf into his arms. "I'll keep her safe, A. You do what you need to do." He headed toward the dune.

Drysi tossed her wand into her left hand and drew a dagger from the vest under her jacket with her right. A light red glow surrounded the blade.

The rumble grew louder. Sand shifted in several places in all directions. A round, segmented body erupted onto the surface and the writhing, dull-scarlet body revealed that it was the front of a worm-like creature. The visible portion was easily longer than two tall men stacked. Jagged teeth circled the front of a gaping mouth that could swallow one of those tall men whole. There was nothing obviously identifiable as eyes on the creature.

Two more of the worms burst from the dunes. They writhed and crawled through the sand to circle the Brownstone team.

Alison exhaled a sigh of relief when she saw that none of the monsters followed Mason and Lily.

She, Drysi, and Hana formed a defensive triangle. Giant

killer worms didn't even make the top ten of strange things they'd fought together.

A sweet, pungent smell suffused the air. She understood what the fox's more sensitive nose had detected.

"Ozone," she muttered.

"Huh?" Drysi frowned. "What does that have to do with anything?"

"That's what they smell like, but I don't know what it means."

Hana watched the monsters, her fingers so tight around the hilt of her weapon that the knuckles whitened. "What the hell are these things? They're totally disgusting."

The worms continued to circle and the pungent odor of ozone grew stronger.

"I'm not sure," their leader replied, "but I think they are Mongolian death worms. Mom's mentioned them a few times but even she wasn't sure if they were real."

"What's their deal?" Hana asked. "Besides smelling funny?"

"There are many contradicting legends. These are far bigger than most of them I've heard tell of and they have all kinds of different abilities in those stories, but they all agree on one thing."

"And what's that?"

"They can attack from a distance."

At least these bastards are patient.

Drysi snorted. "Fucking wonderful. Will we simply stand here and wait for them to kill us?"

Alison shook her head. "I think we should all run at the same time and break their formation. Does that sound good?"

"It's fine with me." A hungry grin pushed the annoyance off Hana's face. "I don't suppose any of the legends say these things are tasty?"

"Tasty? Huh?"

"I'm a little hungry and I want something more than stupid energy bars," the fox complained.

"Most legends say they are poisonous," her friend explained.

Hana stuck her bottom lip out. "Is it too much to expect that a giant killer worm might be a little tasty?"

"Let's focus on killing them before we worry about eating them." She took a deep breath and shunted magical energy into her legs. "Four, three, two, one, go!"

She released the energy and bounded toward the side of a massive dune. One of the death worms broke formation and whipped wildly in pursuit at a surprising speed. She pointed her left palm backward and fired a bolt of light magic. It struck the body of the creature and charred it.

At least these monsters aren't immune to magic, and they don't look like they're regenerating much.

Hana burst toward a gap between two of the death worms. Drysi didn't move. She raised her arm and tilted her dagger. Two of the monsters raised their top segments and swayed as they turned to track the fox. Blue-white arcs of energy crackled inside their mouths.

Oh, shit. That explains the ozone.

The Welsh witch flung her dagger toward the back of what passed for one of the worm's head. It struck and swallowed the exposed body in an orange-red cloud of flame and dark smoke. Hana continued to run. The other worm jerked toward Drysi and ejected a juddering bolt of white-blue electricity. The attack struck her and she careened back with a grunt. She landed and rolled several times but managed to retain a firm grasp on her wand.

She darted to her feet, her shirt and vest blackened slightly. "Right. They spit lightning. Fucking hell."

The smoke cleared from around the victim of the exploding dagger. The acrid scent of its burnt hide mixed with the ozone. It swayed more slowly in an almost hypnotic undulation.

Hana pivoted and launched herself toward the unwounded death worm with a bloodthirsty scream. Her blade moved rapidly as she sliced through the top of the body several times. Bloodied segments plopped on the sand. The remaining body twitched for a few seconds before it sagged and lay still.

Drysi grinned and tossed another explosive dagger into the mouth of her previous victim. The detonation blew the head off to leave another writhing, twitching mass that survived for only a few brief moments.

Alison decided to finish the deadly trifecta. She stopped running and attacked the pursuing death worm. Her blade arced down and sliced the creature's head and its body in half. Electricity surged through the corpse to discharge in an uneven stream above the defeated monster.

She jumped back, waiting for an explosion, but none came. The halves of the monster fell to the bloodstained stand.

"Huh." Drysi tucked her wand back in her holster. "They weren't so bad."

"They're totally gross," Hana insisted and stared at the

chunks of worm with her face contorted in disgust. "I think I prefer the giant roaches."

The Drow walked over and nudged her death worm's corpse. She'd fought more than a few things that could regenerate with ease. For that matter, she could, so she knew better than to ignore the possibility.

"Do you smell anything, Hana?" she asked.

The fox nodded. "I smell many things, but it's probably only from these three. It hasn't become stronger if that's what you're asking."

Alison turned toward Mason. He'd stopped moving in the distance and still carried Lily. She could get stuck looking into the future for minutes at a time and even worse sometimes. It was an inconvenience under normal circumstances, but it could be deadly during a tomb raid. When they'd first met, she didn't have the limitation, but her ability to see into the future was also far more restricted and erratic. Training and experimentation had led to the present situation but it was uncertain if it was a good trade-off.

Drysi snorted. "The stupid worms should have left us alone."

"If we were simply normal people wandering the desert, or even if we were soldiers," Alison began, "we would probably be dead now." She gestured toward the Welshwoman. "Some of that little lightning attack got through Drysi's shield."

Hana sheathed her sword. "In other words, we're totally awesome."

"We are." The witch grinned.

Their boss laughed. "Come on. Let's catch up with

Mason before more worms join the party."

———

Lily sighed, her cheeks scarlet. She stared into the sand. "I'm sorry. That was about the worst time to lose control."

Alison waved a hand, dismissive of her friend's concern. "We did fine, Lily, and that power has saved you, Mom, and me more than a few times. I won't complain because it isn't one hundred percent effective."

Hana pointed at Lily, a look of mock horror on her face. "The Gray Elf curse of the disgusting giant creature magnet! I demand you remove it."

Lily rolled her eyes. "If you think giant worms and roaches are bad, you should see some of what I've run into during my ocean jobs. Pure nightmare fuel."

Mason nodded toward the death worm corpses in the distance. "They're probably not the only ones that we'll encounter."

Alison squinted at the sun hanging high in the sky. "Without our gear, if we stay overnight, we might need to stay in the tomb."

"That has to be the worst hotel ever," Hana commented. "I bet they don't even have a continental breakfast."

Drysi snickered. "I've slept in worse places than tombs."

The Drow shook her head. "I don't even want to know."

She pulled the gem out of her pocket. The arrow was now solid without even a hint of its earlier tenuous nature. "And we're almost there. We've been shot down and attacked by Mongolian death worms. We're due a little luck."

CHAPTER TWELVE

The bright arrow spun and Alison stared at the gem. A dearth of dunes in the area reinforced her initial conclusion after the remainder of their hike.

"I think we're here."

Hana looked around and laughed. "You'd think there would be something more important marking this place—maybe a giant statue or a big monument."

Lily shook her head. "Not necessarily. Like I mentioned on our way here, given the location and some of the background information, this might be the tomb of Genghis Khan. After they buried him, his loyalists went out of their way to make sure his tomb wasn't found, including killing the people who knew where it was. Archaeologists found his palace in the early 2000s, but even though there are many people who have been seeking this since then, no one's ever confirmed it. This would be a really out of the way place to bury him given where his center of Mongol power was at that time, but maybe that was the idea. If they stuck him in the middle of nowhere, people would be less likely to find him."

"Genghis Khan, huh?" Drysi snickered. "There's a man who made the Seventh Order look pleasant."

Hana turned in a slow circle as if the Mongol hordes might appear at any moment and sweep down upon the Brownstone team. "Was he a magical?"

"Not that I've heard." Lily looked thoughtful. "But there were many secret magicals throughout history, so we can't rule it out."

Alison frowned. "If he wasn't a magical, he definitely had some helping him, and considering the job, it might mean that Mr D's nephew was one of them for whatever reason."

Mason eyed her, a subtle expression on his face. She'd long since learned that was his "I'm worried about my woman, but I'm also worried that she'll be annoyed if I say anything face." He'd made it more now that they were married.

"What is it?" she asked him.

He nodded at the gem. "What happens if it turns out this gnome's really bloodthirsty or something? Genghis Khan didn't become famous because he was great at Parcheesi."

"I'm not here to make any kind of historical decision. Mr D has had many opportunities to screw me over, and he hasn't. This might be his bad nephew or maybe, for all we know, Genghis Khan had to kill a number of people to stop an invasion of the Tapestry back in the day. For now, the job stays the same. We'll find the nephew and get his uncle here. After that, I'll let Mr D handle everyone else."

"Understood."

"Everyone, get ready. I'll open the tomb."

Alison lifted the gem and waited as her team raised fresh defensive spells and readied their weapons. She took a deep breath. The gnome had said the language didn't matter, only the intent of her words.

"What has been sealed should be open," she yelled. "What has been lost should be found."

Pulsating, blinding shafts of light poured from the gem. The rays streamed all around the team and formed a kaleidoscopic dome. The ground shook so badly, it tumbled them while staggering waves of magic pulsed from beneath them.

"I think that means it's working," Alison shouted. "Or it could mean we're about to die."

"I hope this doesn't mean a bigger worm is coming," Hana responded as she stood and spread her feet to steady herself. She lifted her sword and the light of her tails and the dome reflected off the blade.

The others managed to stand. They looked around for the ridiculous super-monster they were convinced was coming.

Lily tilted her head for a moment and her lips parted. Her hand grasped her gun lightly. "We should be okay. I've seen what we need to do. It'll only take a minute so hold on."

"You didn't need to do that," Alison insisted, worried that her friend would be caught in the future again. She glanced at the dome. They had no idea about the nature of the magic involved. If they attempted to act mindlessly or without the necessary caution, a spell might kill someone.

It's time to trust Lily. She might get stuck but it's never seemed like her power was wrong.

Alison still held the gem in her palm. It stopped emitting light, but the intensity of the tremors increased and sand shifted in the distance. She conjured a shadow blade, ready to gut whatever mammoth death worm emerged from the ground and tried to eat them.

Something poked out of the sand a few yards away, too angular to be a death worm—dark, worn stone. The movement was slower, too, a few inches a second rather than the sudden eruption she'd witnessed earlier.

Wait. That's not a monster.

It was some kind of angled gateway leading into a stone chamber.

Where did they get the stone? Or was it all conjured?

The structure continued to rise and the shaking and vertical motion loosened the sand from it. An intricate curved vertical script decorated the left and right sides of the rising gateway. The writing pulsed a dull blue. She had no idea how to read it, but she'd worry about translation spells once she was sure an ancient dragon wasn't about to eat them. There were several more lines on the right than the left.

A minute after the dome appeared, it vanished once again and the shaking stopped. The tall, wide gateway could have accommodated an NBA player or a Kilomea with ease, but a shimmering red field blocked the entrance.

The gem crumbled into dust. A light breeze spread the pieces over the nearby sand where they sparkled in the sunlight.

"Is everyone all right?" Alison released her sword and dusted sand and gem remnants off her pants.

Hana sheathed her *tachi* and stared at the gateway. "This isn't a situation where the tomb is in like a different dimension, is it? I can't decide if that would be awesome or freaky."

Drysi grinned. "I'm sure those Tapestry bastards are waiting on the other side to wear us like suits."

Lily removed a small glass sphere from her pocket, the inner surface coated with a dark brown-red substance. It resembled a marble. "Everyone, stand back."

The group complied and the Gray Elf hurled the sphere into the red field. It disappeared with a bright flash.

Mason frowned. "What was that about?"

She pointed to some of the writing. "I can read that, for the most part. On the side, it warns, 'Only when blood is spilled can one pass through the gates.' I carry a little of my dried blood precisely for this kind of situation. You'd be surprised how many spells and wards you can beat with creative thinking."

Hana stuck her tongue out. "That's totally creepy and gross."

"You saw what happens if someone goes in without it in your vision, didn't you?" Alison asked.

Lily nodded. "Yes. That's what I'd call gross."

Drysi smirked and gestured toward the gate. "You don't mind going first then, do you?"

"No problem." The elf winked. "I have confidence in my abilities."

Alison stepped toward the gateway and studied the

writing in greater detail. "None of this looks like any magical or Oriceran script I'm familiar with."

"It's a type of old Mongolian script," Lily explained. "I actually wouldn't expect it to be on Genghis Khan's tomb, but it's not like all linguistic records and theories are always that precise. Still, it's definitely human in origin and not Oriceran." She narrowed her eyes and took a moment to read it again and sighed when finished. "And it doesn't matter because this isn't his tomb."

"That says what it is?" Alison asked and gestured to the script.

"Kind of. It says it is a *chötgör* prison."

Hana groaned. "Please don't tell me that's ancient Mongolian for giant cockroach."

Lily shook her head. "I wish. It's complicated to explain without much background on their native beliefs. They are kind of like minor demons or spirits. I suppose imp's a decent word to use in English. Sometimes, they are supposed to be almost like the undead. In other cases, more like what we would think of as a spirit or demon, but it's wrapped up in local religious and cultural beliefs." She gestured to the inscriptions. "This says, 'After a great and blood-filled incident, there were many men who became imps. The wisest ones say it was because of the dark star that fell and the unholy beast that arose from the crater. The greatest among men, the Great Khan, led a force of powerful warriors and shamans to drive this dark army back. Most of the men fell in the battle, but their sacrifice sealed the imps and the great beast here."

"Wonderful vacation spot," Drysi mused. "I won't lie, I

still prefer the tropical island, even if turned out it was full of homicidal dryads."

Lily winced. "Damn it. Why didn't I realize it before?"

They all spun toward her, their faces strained with worry.

"What now?" Alison asked.

"Kut. It's another name for *chötgör*." The elf groaned. "Please don't tell me your client hired us to bring out someone who's already corrupted."

Hana shrugged. "Maybe his nephew was trying to be ironic with the name?"

Alison pinched the bridge of her nose. "I feel like we have to find this Kut right away. If there's a super-monster hidden here and the Shadows of Rurik arrive, he might know what we need to do to make sure it stays buried."

Mason gave her a worried look. "And if he's a weird, corrupted spirit vampire-like creature?"

"Then we do what we need to do to protect people." She blew out a breath. "Why does everything need to end up so complicated?"

CHAPTER THIRTEEN

Hana sniffed a few times. "This place smells like the ass of a Mountain Strider crossed with rotting mushrooms."

Drysi laughed. "What does the ass of a Mountain Strider smell like, Alison?"

"I wasn't concentrating on funny smells when I fought one," she replied and shook her head slightly. "And this place has been underground for a while. It's not like it would smell like cinnamon."

"Now I'm hungry for a muffin." The fox sighed.

"Fuck the muffin." The Welshwoman grimaced. "I want a damned steak."

Alison chuckled. "We'll survive without a fancy meal for a day. Eat one of your bars if you're hungry."

"You should see what it's like when I have to do a long raid." Lily grimaced and clutched her stomach. "It's rare, but there's nothing more obnoxious than being stuck in the middle of nowhere without any decent hot food. MREs and bars simply aren't the same. I'm still a city girl at heart." She grinned at Alison. "Even if I was never as prissy as some."

Her friend rolled her eyes. "That was a long time ago, Lily."

Mason smirked and opened his mouth to speak but shut it when Alison gave him a death stare—the kind only a wife could manage.

They walked down a slowly widening tunnel. The soft illumination of their light orbs and flashlights killed the darkness, including the surprising brightness of Hana's tails. The light revealed nothing but smooth stone walls, and the occasional inscription reiterated the location's status as an imp prison.

I wonder if Mr D was more worried about the Shadows of Rurik than he was about this place. It's not been too bad so far.

Drysi scowled into the darkness. "Isn't this all too simple?" she asked.

"What do you mean?" Alison asked, uncomfortable with the synchronicity of thought.

"It's a prison. Shouldn't it have cells or artifacts or something?" The witch shrugged. "It's only an entrance and a big tunnel. And I haven't seen anything that looks like a nasty little monster, either."

"Maybe they all broke out a long time ago," Hana suggested with an excited gleam in her eyes. "And they turned to sand when exposed to the light, forming the Gobi Desert."

"I'm reasonably sure the desert is a little older than that," Alison countered. "And that would have taken millions of imps."

Mason looked over his shoulder, suspicion in his eyes.

"I've wondered the same thing as Drysi. I thought these kinds of places were more elaborate—tombs and ancient prisons and ancient palaces."

Lily shook her head. "That's the mistake many people make. They project modern urban architecture ideas into the past. Yes, there can be elaborate structures with tons of hallways and rooms, but most of the places were much simpler and certainly smaller. On my average raid, it's the traps and guardians that are the trouble, not navigation. Not every site will be a labyrinth."

Alison nodded. "Mom told me that, too. The whole super-elaborate Lara Croft/Caleb Rodriguez-style mazes are the exceptions rather than the rule. It usually took her more time to do the background research than to do her initial exploration on many of the raids, but at least it was a place that was still standing and not buried under fifty feet of sand."

"Exactly." The Gray Elf grinned. "And we tomb raiders tend to target the low-hanging fruit when possible. If it requires a hundred grad students with tiny shovels, it's not a practical job, especially if we're playing fast and loose with the whole, 'Is it even legal?' question."

The Drow narrowed her eyes as the light revealed something new. A stone column stretched from the floor and all the way to the ceiling. While it blocked their direct path ahead, the walkway curved into two paths, one on either side. The team continued, their pace slower than before.

Hundreds of small glowing symbols reminiscent of the earlier ancient Mongolian writing covered the column from the top to the bottom. The symbols followed the curve of the structure, leaving no side untouched. They pulsed slowly from red to green following a smooth color gradient over several seconds before repeating the process. A few larger symbols ringed the bottom and top. The entire column radiated high levels of magic. Strangely, they'd barely been able to sense it until they were only a few yards away.

Drysi gestured to the column. "What's with that?" She looked at the elf for an explanation. "An ancient Mongolian Christmas tree?"

Hana snickered.

"I'm reasonably sure that's not the case," Lily responded. She circled either side of the column and shook her head. "But I don't know exactly what it's supposed to be. These aren't intelligible words. I don't think this is language, not in the sense that they directly wanted to communicate something." She took a deep breath and stared at the column for a moment before she exhaled slowly. "I didn't see anything strange happening."

Alison took a step closer and stared at the symbols. Not every type of magic was compatible or based on the same fundamental principles, which made it difficult to identify certain spells at a glance. Still, a combination of her practical experience on the job, her time at the School of Necessary Magic, and her Drow training allowed her to venture an educated guess.

Your joke about the Mountain Strider might have helped me this time, Iluna.

She pointed at the column. "I think those are containment wards but they aren't like any I've seen before."

"Master control for the imps?" Hana asked. She leaned

closer, her vulpine gaze slowly moving up and down as she scanned the length of the column.

"Probably something like that."

Mason's brow wrinkled with worry. "If that's what they are, they don't feel or look like they're failing."

"That's a good thing." Alison shrugged. "We're here to free Kut, not the imps."

"Is it a good thing?" Drysi drew a dagger. "We could blow the whole thing."

"And release the imps?" She watched the other woman, looking for some sign of humor, but the witch's expression remained serious.

"At least we get it over with and clean the little bastards out." The Welshwoman tucked the dagger into one of her vest sheaths. "There's a good chance we'll have to fight them if we don't turn around and march out the front again."

Mason gestured the way they had come. "The inscription said before it needed the Great Khan and his greatest warriors and shamans. I'm not sure we want to purposefully pick that kind of fight."

Drysi scoffed. "He probably had an army of guys without magic and one gnome. We have our primary team here. If Alison can defeat a Mountain Strider that smells like ass by herself, we can win with her plus the rest of us."

"I didn't defeat the Mountain Strider," Alison insisted. "All I did was reseal it. And it didn't smell all that much that I can remember."

Wait. Why am I even commenting on that?

"Merely being in here might mess with these wards,"

Mason observed. Tension lined his forehead. "We have to consider risk versus reward here."

Alison sighed. "Yeah, I know. I've thought about pulling out, but I have the feeling it's too late. If the Shadows or anyone else arrives, they might want to open the prison anyway."

"Why would they want to do that?" Hana asked.

"Think about the kind of crap the Seventh Order pulled, and not only the Mountain Strider." She glared at the column as if blaming the defeated dark wizards for it. "Some people don't care about collateral damage."

"All the more reason to bring it on and blow those little bastards away." Drysi offered her a vicious grin. "The death worms weren't so hard. How bad could the imps be?"

She might still be a little bloodthirsty but wanting to kill imps isn't awful.

Lily coughed to clear her throat. "I'm using imp here in the sense of a demon of limited magical ability. I don't mean they're literally tiny little creatures like you might see in a movie. I don't think we should underestimate how dangerous they might be."

"We won't deliberately try to fight them. Not yet." Alison layered another shield over herself. "Once we find and free Kut, we'll consult with him on the best way to prevent this place from causing trouble. He would know. Drysi's partially right."

"You're damned right, I am." The Welsh witch raised her chin and squared her shoulders.

"What I'm getting at is that the gates are open now," the Drow explained. "There's simply more magic floating around Earth. It might be far easier for us to fight these things than an ancient wizard who hadn't been to a kemana for a while."

"That's quite a few assumptions, A," Mason commented.

"Sure, but that doesn't make them wrong." She retrieved the small candle from her pocket and frowned at an unexpected sight.

A ghostly lavender flame flickered from the top of it, barely present but definitely noticeable.

"A, were you on fire?" He frowned in sudden concern.

Hana sniffed. "I don't smell anything like that."

Alison shook her head. "I didn't feel a thing. I pulled it out simply to make sure we had it." She reached into the pocket and felt around. There was no sign of any damage so she placed her hand over the flame.

Hana grimaced. "Woah, there."

It was cool to the touch.

"It doesn't hurt," she explained.

"Maybe it's like the gem," the fox suggested. "It might get brighter the closer we are to him."

"I don't like the fact that this is already alight. It seems like Mr D didn't understand the implications of all this as much as he thought he did."

Mason frowned. "Do you think he purposefully kept things from you?"

Alison shook her head. "No, I don't. I do think he cares more about his nephew than he let on, and that made him sloppy. This was probably more rushed than he would normally have liked."

Lily circled the column again slowly. "Even if this isn't Genghis Khan's tomb, it's from that era. We're talking about eight centuries ago. Even a gnome can't be the master of all magic after centuries."

Irritation etched itself onto Alison's face. "It's not the first time a client was overeager and didn't do enough background research. We press on for now. Those two pilots already died, and that wasn't Mr D's fault. I would prefer their deaths weren't wasted. If Hana's right, this candle will help even more than we realized." She tucked it into her pocket again. "Let's move on." She glanced at the column one last time before she moved around to the right and back to the tunnel leading deeper.

Mason and Lily walked on either side of her. Drysi and Hana brought up the rear. Although everyone had their defensive artifacts and spells active, no one had a weapon out.

More writing confronted them on one side of the tunnel, along with odd artwork that resembled charcoal outlines of the upper half of people.

I'm surprised that lasted so well after hundreds of years, but this place isn't exposed to the outside, so maybe that's why. It's not even all that dusty. My house gets dustier than this place.

"The dark star fell," Lily translated. "And threatened to swallow the entire world. Let all who are unworthy join the imps."

Hana glared at the wall. "What's that supposed to mean?"

"I'm not sure." The Gray Elf shrugged. "Sometimes, the creatures described could possess people in certain legends, and the earlier inscription said people became imps. They could be talking about something like that."

Drysi rolled her eyes. "It's probably all bullshit propaganda. If they were so tough and saved the world, why haven't I heard about it before?"

"At a time when magic was suppressed?" Alison shook her head. "It's one thing to say you have a few shamans helping you, but that's different than openly trumpeting the heavy use of magic all over the world. Advertising a place like this to evil magicals is merely asking for trouble."

"Why bother with all these inscriptions then?"

She pointed to one of their light orbs. "Finding this required magic. They did want to brag, but only if the right kind of people came along first."

"Duck!" Lily commanded.

Everyone dropped to their stomachs without question or thought. Streams of black liquid hissed at eye-level from the walls and continued for several seconds before they stopped. A few droplets fell to the ground and sizzled.

The team crawled forward several yards.

"Now what?" Alison muttered.

The Gray Elf blew out a breath. "We should be okay."

"You saw the future?" she asked.

Lily shook her head and pointed behind them to part of the uneven stone floor that was slightly recessed. "I try to be careful about that since I've been lost there a little more recently than normal. There's a pressure plate." She inclined her head toward the wall. "And only the tops of the bodies are displayed on the walls. I think that's what they were getting at with having to join the imps. I didn't want to test if our defenses were good enough to take the hit."

Hana rolled her eyes. "Stupid ancient Mongolian death traps. Giant worms. Exploding planes. It's like this entire country is trying to kill us. No wonder they don't have a Starbucks. I'm offended, both as a security contractor and a Seattleite."

Alison stood slowly. "Even if we could have taken the magic train, we would still have had to fly to this site. For now, let's proceed slowly." She cast a suspicious glance at the ground before she opened her pocket to check the candle. The flame didn't appear brighter than before. "It looks like we still have a little hike ahead of us."

CHAPTER FOURTEEN

Lily's careful perception and excellent research helped the team avoid two more traps.

The tunnel widened to the point that they could have driven a decent-sized tank through without much difficulty. Despite the mild angle of decline, it was clear the team had traveled deep underground. The fetid stench of rotting corpses grew stronger the farther they progressed, but they hadn't seen any sign of the source. If anything, everything was too clean.

Their trip finally brought them into a huge rectangular chamber. Five other columns stood inside, similar to the one they had encountered earlier. Their wards pulsed at a slow speed, exactly as they had on the first pillar. Another tunnel opened on the opposite side of the chamber.

Again, the smell of rotting bodies filled their nostrils, but there were no corpses, no bones, nor any hint that anything or anyone had been in the room in centuries.

"What the hell is that smell?" the Drow complained.

Hana stuck her tongue out and shook her head. "Nasty. That's what it is."

Alison checked the candle, which now featured a much brighter flame, but it wasn't any hotter than before.

"At least we're getting closer," she declared. "I hope so, at least."

Hana tilted her head and peered at the candle. "If it's already alight, does that mean Mr D is coming? You were supposed to summon him with it, right?"

"That was the plan, but we also didn't plan to get shot out of the sky on our way here." She ran her hand through the cool flame a few times. "I think if I actually try to light it, there will be a different kind of flame. We'll worry about it when we find Kut, assuming he's not a charcoal drawing on the wall at this point."

She'd made sure to check the heights of earlier humanoid forms. All of them were clearly taller than a gnome.

If he used magic to change his shape to human, would he end up like that on the wall?

Mason narrowed his eyes and looked from column to column, his obvious suspicion building with each passing second. He pointed to the middle column. "Is it only me or are the lights speeding up?"

Drysi yanked out two explosive knives. "That can't be good." Her excited tone and huge smile undermined her words.

Hana drew her sword. "Does this mean more of that weird disintegration spray is coming? I'd rather not end up turned into crappy wall art. If I die, I want a sexy statue made out of me."

"Don't put in your request for a sculptor yet." Alison tucked the candle into her pocket before she conjured a shadow blade. She watched the columns for a few seconds to confirm Mason's observations. "I hate to risk it but Lily, can you take a look?"

The other woman took a deep breath and drew her gun. She didn't respond and instead, she stared ahead and her eyes glazed over.

"Damn it," Alison muttered. "I think we lost her."

The color cycling on the wards increased speed with an unnatural, almost electronic look to the display. There was no sound and no rumble. The background magic in the area didn't feel any different.

Lily stumbled back and shook her head a couple of times with a gasp. "I'm still here, Alison. I was trying to be thorough. Trouble's coming—a heap of trouble. I'm not sure, but I think it's the imps or something equally as nasty."

Mason drew his gun, his expression grim. "We should have left when we had the chance."

Hana chopped at the air a few times. "It's nice to get a little exercise, but we could run."

Alison shook her head and raised her hand. She channeled light and dark magic into her palm, slowly building an orb of destruction. "If we're responsible for the prison break, we're also responsible for taking care of the prisoners. Everyone, take position near the entrance."

Drysi looked disappointed. "We are running then?"

"Merely positioning ourselves strategically."

The wards turned black, leaving the team's orbs and flashlights to cut through the shadows. There wasn't enough light for the large room and the far corners were choked in inky darkness. Alison's stomach lurched at the magical pressure that emanated from the columns, but she continued to fuel her spell.

This Kut better not be an asshole, Mr D.

"Attacking the puddles won't do any good," Lily shouted. "I've already seen it."

"What puddles?" Hana asked.

Streams of thick black liquid swirled from the pillars, despite the lack of obvious spouts or holes. The flows ended in different locations and fueled dark puddles. More erupted from the source and the small number of puddles grew into dozens in less than thirty seconds.

"Oh, those puddles." The fox grimaced

Alison concentrated on containing the magical energy in her spell but ceased adding more. If she charged it too much and launched it, she risked burying her entire team under hundreds of feet of dirt and sand.

"Come on, you bastards," Drysi shouted. "Someone already tried to blow me up today. I doubt you little fuckers have much to offer." She shot an angry glare at Lily. "Are you sure we can't attack the puddles?"

"Hey, I'm only telling you what I saw," the Gray Elf retorted.

The dozens of shallow pools soon became scores, but the flows stopped. Ripples appeared in the liquid as if a giant beast stamped on the ground nearby, but they didn't feel anything and the magical pressure lessened. She continued to maintain the balance of the magic in her orb.

Sparkling steam rose from the puddles. A few seconds later, the vapor erupted in a bright flash accompanied by a loud pop. Another followed, then others in rapid succession. The overlapping of the echoing din assaulted their ears.

Drysi shouted a stream of profanities, half in English and half in Welsh.

Alison scowled and narrowed her eyes, her vision blurry from so many flashes. The liquid had vanished. Gray emaciated humanoid shapes stood in their place, covered with cracked, leathery skin. Their two overly long arms ended in sharp, blackened claws. Between their round ears and their toothless mouths, one could see that they might have once been humans. Their yellow eyes reflected the light of the flashlights and orbs. Black bones protruded from their back, a few scraps of atrophied muscle and rotted skin on them, mockeries of what could have been wings.

Huh. Maybe we got lucky. Did these guys use to be much worse?

With a choir of hisses, the monsters swept into a loping attack toward the Brownstone team.

And there we go.

Alison thrust her hand forward and launched her orb. It surged and crackled across the chamber before it detonated on contact with the front line of the horde. The room shook from the explosion. Dirt and rock dropped from the ceiling.

Maybe not so many of those.

Drysi cackled. "Now we're talking." She flung a dagger to either side of Alison's target. Two smaller blasts seared into the imp front line and flung pieces of the creatures like desiccated shrapnel.

Survivors continued their approach and closed in on Alison. Lily and Mason opened fire. Their bullets struck the imps in the chest. The aggressors jerked back but a few seconds later, the bullet wounds sealed themselves.

A legless imp crawled out of the smoke of the explosion, mere stumps beneath him that immediately began to lengthen and widen into new legs.

"That's not fair," Hana declared. "Die already."

"Not all of them survived," Alison observed. "There has to be a way to win other than blowing them completely to pieces. If we try that, we'll end up sucking sand." She whipped her arm out and launched a shadow crescent. The magical attack sliced into an imp's chest and he careened into another group of advancing enemies, but his regeneration began before his momentum even slowed.

Lily drew her magic dagger with her left hand while she squeezed off a headshot at the nearest imp. It stumbled back only for the wound to seal itself in seconds.

Drysi frowned. She stowed her gun, yanked her wand from the holster, and shouted a fireball spell. The blaze exploded against an enemy, charred it, and knocked it into a heap. It sat up immediately and new flesh began to grow over the blackened burns.

Mason ejected his magazine and shoved in one with anti-magic rounds. He squeezed off two quick shots into the head of an imp. It fell forward and didn't regenerate.

"At least that worked," Alison commented.

"I don't have enough anti-magic rounds to kill this many," he complained.

Jerry's teams might carry a large supply of that type of

ammo, but Alison was used to being able to defeat magical enemies using her own magic.

An attacker on the far end lunged at Hana. She cut it in half with a single stroke, but the monster continued to reach for her. She growled and decapitated it with her next blow. It stopped moving.

"Separate the head from the neck," she shouted. She surged forward, a wide, hungry grin on her face, and sliced with abandon. "Take this, you freaks!"

That works.

The Drow summoned another shadow blade and sprinted into the monsters to twirl, thrust, and cut. A few clawed at her shields, but her defenses held. Their necks didn't survive her counterattacks.

Lily kept her gun ready but ceased fire, gritting her teeth. Mason pointed his wand to Alison's side and combined a murmur with a few quick motions. Chunks of stone ripped from the floor and smashed into the aggressors and tumbled them. His wife followed up a moment later and sliced through their necks before the monsters could even find their feet.

Hana's *tachi* swung in relentless arcs, the light of her tails highlighting the rear lines of the enemy. She continued to run as she carved through the ranks. Drysi maintained her fireball support and mostly concentrated on pounding their opponents in the back. They stumbled with each attack, which delayed them from swarming the butchering nine-tailed fox.

Alison hacked and chopped through more of the creatures. She could see how a Mongol horse archer with a normal sword might have trouble against a regenerating monster that felt no pain or fear, but her shadow blades sliced through the imp necks with ease. The huge number of enemies quickly fell to dozens and soon, the dozens to less than ten.

Hana joined her and they rushed toward the survivors from opposite sides. Their blades only paused to change direction. The imps fell, headless, and remained motionless.

"I win!" Hana shouted as the *tachi* decapitated the final foe. "I'm totally sure I killed more than you did."

Alison chuckled and released one of her blades. "Sure, whatever. You win. Is everyone all right?"

Drysi kicked at an imp corpse. "What the hell?"

Everyone turned toward her. A faint hiss preceded cracks that rippled through the body. The corpse began to disintegrate in a cloud of thick smoke. The others began to do the same.

Their leader pointed her blade at the tunnel on the far side. "Don't breathe, just in case. Let's go!"

CHAPTER FIFTEEN

The team rushed away from the imp smoke into another tunnel, half-expecting the entire room to explode. They made it about thirty yards before Alison bothered to check the walls for any writing or people's outlines on the wall. She glanced at Lily. Her friend nodded, and the entire group slowed to a jog and stopped.

She took a deep breath. "This is why I didn't follow in Mom's footsteps."

The Gray Elf chuckled. "Because bounty hunting is so much safer?"

"It can be. In theory."

Mason looked at the smoke-filled chamber with a frown. "There were bigger wards on that earlier monument. That might not mean anything, or it might mean we still have more trouble coming."

"Giant zombie imps?" Hana laughed. "This gets better." She patted the hilt of her blade. "I always wanted to do the whole run up the giant monster action."

Lily shook her head. "We have to be careful. We don't

know what might happen. Those wards might be related to something else entirely."

"The great beast," Alison suggested. "That's what the inscription said, right?"

The elf nodded grimly. "That's what I'd guess, and we have no idea what it might be. I doubt it's merely a giant imp."

"For now, let's find the gnome. Once Mr D gets here, we can figure out everything else."

"And if a giant imp attacks us before then?" Drysi asked.

"Then we destroy it." Alison pulled the candle out of her pocket. The flame now burned brightly. "Let's hope Kut can help fill in the blanks once his uncle wakes him up." She continued down the hallway, holding the candle in front of her.

The tunnel narrowed and they arrived at a steep, narrow stone staircase only wide enough for a single person. A bright light shone at the bottom of the stairs, easily hundreds of feet down.

Hana peered at the stairs. "Trap much?"

Drysi frowned. "I don't get it. They would have needed all kinds of magic to build a place like this in the middle of the desert."

"You already pointed it out, Drysi." Alison gestured to the walls. "This isn't a complicated layout. If they had a few transmutation specialists, it would have been even easier. The wards are probably the most complicated spells here." She inclined her head toward the candle. "I'm willing to bet that's Kut down there."

Mason raised an eyebrow. "And if it's the beast?"

"Then I'll kill it, and we'll keep looking for Kut." She moved toward the first step, but Lily grabbed her shoulder.

Her friend shook her head. "Your defenses might be stronger, but my reflexes are better, and if I don't go crazy with my precognition, it should be okay."

"Are you sure? If you freeze, it's a long fall."

"My artifact can take it. I survived a plane crash, remember?" She placed her foot on the first step. "I think you should wait up here until I'm at the bottom. If there's a trap, it'll be harder for everyone to dodge in such a narrow space."

"Fine," Alison replied but tension lined her voice. "Don't die. You don't even get an artifact out of this. It's not worth you risking too much."

"That's what friends are for, right? Risking their lives in dangerous holes in the ground." Lily chuckled and took a few tentative steps. "Yes, helping you out always seems to involve something ridiculously lethal." She lowered her head a little so her headlamp's beam pierced the darkness to reveal more stairs. "Give me a few minutes. I want to be the tortoise, not the hare."

"I could fly down," the Drow countered. "If they use pressure plates, I doubt they accounted for someone flying."

The Gray Elf glanced from her to the bottom of the stairs. "They might have taken that into account and it's not that wide." She waved confidently. "I'll be right back. You don't always have to volunteer to be the martyr, Alison."

Mason looked relieved.

Alison folded her arms and waited as her friend

descended the steep, slick staircase. Her footfalls echoed up the narrow stairway, making her sound like a Kilomea rather than a slender Gray Elf.

No one spoke during the tomb raider's cautious advance. They all watched the stairs in tense silence with only thumping hearts and breathing to distract them. A few minutes later, Lily's light was almost indistinguishable from the illumination at the bottom of the stairway.

"Alison," Lily shouted. "You should get down here. It's not the beast, and I think we'll need the candle."

Shadow wings sprouted from Alison's back. She released a sigh of relief. "Go ahead and stay here. I'll take care of this." She swooped into the stairwell, the candle in hand.

I invited Lily along knowing full well how dangerous this would be. I'm in the wrong line of business if I can't handle that kind of thing.

Her friend was right. The space was too narrow to accommodate her normal wings, immaterial though they were, but she didn't need to turn. She only needed to fall in a controlled manner, and they acted more like magical thrusters than true wings anyway. She descended rapidly and the glow at the bottom brightened with each passing second. A quick twist at the last moment stopped her from colliding with Lily in the tiny round chamber at the base.

The other woman stood in front of a glowing humanoid form that floated in the back of the room below some inscribed text. Even though the bright white light obscured most of the details, the size and shape were both consistent with a gnome. The candle's flame roared like a gas torch, the fire now twice as long as its source.

Alison pointed to the text. "What does it say?"

"The great shaman sacrificed to stop the beast," Lily related. She gestured to the candle. "Now what? It's already on fire."

She raised her hand and concentrated a little magical power around the candle until fire bathed the entire length of the candle. Carefully, she set the purple wax down and backed away. The flames roared and reached several feet in the air like the candle had become an out-of-control firework. Heat filled the previously chilly underground chamber. Fire surged from the candle and spread over the floating form. The light vanished to reveal a bald gnome in a ragged and torn brown robe.

Lily stood as if transfixed, her pupils dilated and her mouth agape.

Damn it. Did you push it too much and get lost again? I hope this isn't about to kill us both. Here lies Alison Brownstone, killed by an exploding gnome.

Alison frowned. The candle was supposed to act as a beacon for Mr D, but she'd long since accepted there was way too much about the job he had wrong or misunderstood. Being ancient and powerful wasn't the same thing as being omniscient.

The flame surrounding the gnome in the chamber cycled through different colors. First red and orange, then green and blue before, with a hiss, the fire extinguished itself and the gnome fell and landed with a soft grunt.

His eyes flickered open, and he looked at Lily and Alison, his face scrunched in confusion. He rattled something off in a language Alison didn't understand. It didn't even sound like a language she had studied from either Oriceran or Earth.

She shrugged. "If that's medieval Mongolian, it's not a language I speak."

The gnome frowned. Disappointment filled his eyes. He sighed and raised his hand. After a series of intricate movements and a quiet chant, he stared at her. "Can you understand me now, Drow?"

He knows I'm a Drow? I have the hair, of course, but I don't have the ears.

"Yes," she answered.

He turned to look at the writing. "Great shaman, huh? This is still Earth?"

She nodded. "Yes. You're in the Gobi Desert, but I don't know what they called it whenever you were stuck here. By the way, if you were helping Genghis Khan, that was a long time ago. Hundreds of years, in fact."

"And why is a Drow rescuing me?" The gnome circled her warily, his eyes narrowed. "Your kind has nothing but derision for non-Drow."

"Half-Drow," she corrected. "And you don't know me, so I won't take that personally, but I'm not a normal Drow. Besides, many things have changed. They don't even have a queen anymore." Even if Laena hadn't likely been alive when the gnome had been sealed, the Drow matriarchy went back thousands of years.

"A half-Drow? And no Drow queen?" He shook his head and the expression on his face suggested it was the most ridiculous thing he'd ever heard.

He pointed at Lily. "And the Gray Elf? I can't think of two races whose fundamental natures are more opposed. Is she your ally?" He scrutinized her carefully. "It seems you've disabled her."

"She's a friend of mine, and she's…" Alison sighed. "I didn't attack or disable her. It's a long story. She'll come out of it soon. Just to be sure, are you Kut?"

"I go by that sometimes. It's convenient enough." He tapped his lip. "Something else feels off as well. Some of the lesser wards have been disrupted." He leaned closer to her. "But it doesn't feel like they've been pulled apart. If anything, it's the opposite. It feels like too much power is flowing into them, and they've ripped. Too much power even for this place. I accounted for that when I set them up. What did you do, Drow?"

"My name isn't Drow. It's Alison Brownstone." She shrugged. "Maybe it's because the gates have begun to open. It's been a few decades since they started. There's more magic on Earth now. Like I said, many things have changed?"

Kut's eyes widened. "And what of Oriceran?"

"It's…there?" Alison sighed. "It's simply Oriceran."

"That explains it, then. If you'd only tampered with the wards, it would have woken me sooner." He tapped his foot and folded his arms. "You still haven't told me why a Drow is helping a gnome other than you're not a normal Drow."

"That's complicated. Magic isn't secret. Look, I'd love to catch you up, but why don't we get out of here first?" She pointed to the stairs. "Actually, it's not that complicated. I'm here because your uncle sent me."

"My uncle?"

"He goes by Mr D now. I have no idea what he went by back in the day."

"Oh. That uncle." The gnome nodded and some of the incredulity faded from his expression. "It makes sense he would help me. I'm surprised he'd send someone like you, but he always was an odd one."

Lily blinked a few times and shook her head. She stared at the gnome. "He's awake?"

"I am," he declared. "Because of you and your Drow friend."

"Your uncle gave us a purple candle," Alison explained, "but it was only supposed to summon him."

Kut laughed. "I can't believe he used one of those. He must have been desperate."

"Wait. What's the deal with the candle?" Alison frowned. "It was supposed to act as a beacon to bring him because of the magical interference in the area."

If Mr D risked my friends, we'll have a Dad-style talk with him.

"It's not dangerous to you if that's what you're worried about. It could have killed him, though." Kut sighed. "But I have my doubts that even a gnome as talented as him will be able to navigate the complexities of the strange magic in this area. But, before we worry about that…" When he snapped his fingers, a stylish suit replaced his robe. "Is this acceptable for the current era?" He looked from one woman to the other. "It doesn't match your clothes, but you are women."

"You're taking this awfully well," Alison commented. "I think if I woke up centuries later, I'd be a little more shocked."

He waved a hand dismissively. "Oh, I'm sure the humans have built their castles higher with the help of wizards, now that everything doesn't have to be kept secret." He ran a hand over his scalp. "But short-lived creatures are always the same, regardless of what fancy coliseum they've built."

Lily smirked. "I think you'd be surprised. Humans have improved things considerably. Flying machines, artificial thinking machines, cotton candy. They've even been to the moon. All without magic."

Kut stared at her with an expression that betrayed an utter lack of comprehension. "I...see." He sighed. "There are things we should discuss."

"Let's go up the stairs," Alison suggested. "And that way, we can brief my entire team at once. I don't know how long it'll take your uncle to get here."

"A witch, a wizard, a Gray Elf, a Drow, and a nine-tailed fox?" Kut burst out laughing. "Earth really is different now."

Hana rolled her eyes. "It's been a long time since you helped Genghis Khan slaughter people, old man."

His smile faded. "If it weren't for me, he would have done far worse, but it doesn't matter because the aid of his warriors was vital for dealing with the more pressing issue here. If we'd not stopped the beast, it might have grown too powerful."

Alison nodded. "What happened, exactly?"

"A meteor fell. It was infused with odd and powerful magic that could be felt far off. There was a powerful entity inside it, something not fully intelligent but frighteningly strong. I became aware of its effects when it transformed an entire village beyond the desert into the corrupted." Kut shook his head. "I allied with other witches and wizards, and we managed to seal the creature and its magic, but only after fighting through armies of the corrupted."

"What was this creature?" Mason asked.

Kut shrugged. "I don't know. We never faced it directly, only sensed it indirectly. We gained some sense of its enormities with attempts to scry it, but we didn't want to press too deeply because of the risk. It never left the meteor, and after we fought through its defenders with the help of the Khan's forces, we sank the meteor deep into the desert and sealed most of the beast's power. Someone needed to maintain the seal, so I volunteered because I wasn't sure the others could survive the spell. They were responsible for taking care of the residual magical power that had corrupted the area. It's ability to change people, even after being sealed, was too much of a risk." He pointed to a wall. "And it appears they built the appropriate place to do that."

Drysi scoffed. "Those freaks weren't so hard to beat. All you had to do was cut their heads off."

The gnome gave her the pitying look one might normally save for a deluded young child. "That was only fortune aiding you. The magic of the beast is strange and different from what you're used to on Earth or Oriceran. When we fought them before, they could come back, even if we burned them to ashes. The centuries must have taken a toll on their power. But you can still be proud of yourself that you defeated something weakened to a bare fragment of its original power." He gave her a pleasant smile.

"We should have left you at the bottom of the stairs," Drysi muttered.

Mason frowned. "Wait a minute. If the wards are failing on the imps, what about the beast?"

Kut held up a hand and closed his eyes. He held his breath for a few seconds before he exhaled. "They're fine. These were created using different principles. The imps are ultimately corrupted Earth people and have a fundamental link to the natural magic of this planet, but the beast is something else. Now that magic has returned to Earth, it's natural repulsion against the creature's magic should make it easier to contain. We merely need to wait for the magical feedback to diminish its power to the point where we can kill it without risking further corruption."

Alison sighed. She knew she wouldn't like the answer, but she had to ask the question anyway. "And how long is that supposed to take?"

"I estimated it at about a thousand years when we sealed it, but if what you're telling me is right, we're almost there. Only a few more centuries." He tugged at the end of his sleeve. "I don't know if I like these new human fashions." He clapped. "But it's no matter. Let's travel to the surface. I'll reinforce the wards from there and wait for my uncle."

Somehow, I don't think it'll be that simple.

CHAPTER SIXTEEN

The team advanced slowly as they returned to the larger chamber. Lily and Alison took the lead. Everyone kept their defenses up and their weapons at the ready, although Kut wandered along with an amused smile on his face, He almost seemed as if he'd woken up from a long nap instead of being asleep for centuries after helping to seal a horrific magical threat. At least he had the decency to throw up a shield spell of his own.

I never will understand gnomes, Alison thought.

She'd met gnomes as old as some of Earth's greatest civilizations who were disturbingly normal. While she didn't know what she wanted, perhaps something more conspicuously sagacious would have satisfied her. After a couple of centuries, she doubted she would be as laid back as someone like Kut or the librarian at the School of Necessary Magic.

"Are you really okay with all this?" she asked him. "Many people you know are dead now, and you've taken waking up in a strange new world surprisingly well."

Alison wasn't sure why she cared so much. Maybe her recent marriage had brought the future into greater focus.

"Such is life." He pointed to the side of his head. "But they're not really dead as long as I remember them. It's always so interesting to me that some races fear death so much, but it's almost always the ones who live shorter lives. But you're a Drow and, from the looks of it, you're what—a hundred? Two hundred? You have centuries left. Why are you so obsessed with death? Other than with the death of your enemies as your people tend to be."

"I'm half-Drow and, uh…" Her cheeks heated. "Let's say I'm far younger than a hundred."

Kut raised an eyebrow. "Oh. Seventy-five?"

"Keep going."

This is ridiculous.

He chuckled. "No wonder you worry so much. I'm surprised at your magical power given that you're a child. I could barely accomplish anything useful when I was that young."

"Thanks. I guess."

Mason stepped toward the gnome, but she shook her head. Her husband stepped back and mumbled under his breath. It was no surprise that an overprotective boyfriend became an overprotective husband.

They arrived and passed through the large dust-filled chamber with the five columns. Thick imp ash coated the walls, but no monsters appeared to attack them. If an archaeologist or tomb raider later investigated, they would never know of the fierce battle waged inside the stone walls.

"One moment." Kut headed over to a column and placed his hand on the surface. Light pulsed through the wards. Those on the other columns illuminated.

Alison frowned and searched the room for new enemies. "What are you doing? We don't need any unnecessary fights on the way out."

"I agree, which is why I'm checking things. I've been away for a long time and I want to make sure everything is still working as intended." The gnome removed his hand and appeared satisfied. "Excellent. It's as I expected. You only temporarily stopped the corrupted, but the wards will hold them before they can reform. I'll have months to redo the wards, and I assume I can find others to help me. If my uncle isn't on his way already, I'll be able to establish contact with him on the surface." He fluffed his lapels. "But let me be clear that I respect how you defeated so many of them with such a small number of people. I had more allies when I faced them, both magical and non-magical."

Okay, at least he can respect talent. That's not so bad.

Alison nodded toward the far exit. "Thanks. Can we get going? If something goes wrong, I'd still rather be on the surface. If necessary, we can bury this place, and that should buy us time until your uncle gets here."

"You were curious about me being unperturbed, but you penetrated a magic prison and faced a large number of dangerous foes, and this is obviously not your land." The corner of Kut's mouth turned up in a smile. "Exactly how often do you do this kind of thing?"

Drysi cackled. "Too damned often."

"I'm a security contractor. It's kind of my job."

"The Mountain Strider you contained wasn't really your job," the fox chimed in with a smile.

The gnome frowned. "A Mountain Strider? On Earth? What fool would dare violate the Great Treaty?"

So we finally found something that worries him. Good. He does take this seriously.

Hana smirked. "Don't worry. We eliminated the bastards responsible." She pointed at Alison. "The wizards, not the Mountain Strider. Alison sealed it."

He rounded on Alison. "Exactly what kind of Drow are you?"

"Princess of the Shadow Forged." Hana bowed. "We're not worthy."

"Oh? Interesting."

"Cut that out, Hana." Her boss frowned. "I have power so I use it to help people. There's nothing wrong with that. My past is complicated. I didn't even know about my magic until I was fifteen. I'm not so different than you."

"I'm not a prince." Kut's merry grin annoyed her.

"You had power and you helped to protect people." She shrugged. "It's not a great mystery. I'm not special."

"If only most with power thought the same, the Great Treaty wouldn't have even been necessary." He offered her a solemn glance before he stepped away from the column. "Let's be off. You're right. We should leave this place and get help."

"That's fine with me."

Despite the continued risk of traps, between Kut and Lily's previous mental mapping, the return journey through the imp prison was far swifter than their initial foray. Alison stopped being surprised by the modest complexity and small number of traps. There was no secret treasure hidden inside the prison, only an easy-going gnome and monsters. The entire structure had remained hidden for centuries. Obscurity might have been the best defense in the end.

She gestured to one of the outlines on the wall as they passed through a tunnel. "Isn't that somewhat harsh?"

"That little touch wasn't mine." The gnome studied the wall with mild disapproval on his face. "My allies must have harbored concerns about short-sighted magicals invading this prison. I doubt any of them are still alive for me to question them." Melancholy touched his voice.

So you're not as cool with the future shock as you let on, huh?

Alison froze as they stepped into the modestly sized chamber that contained the single stone column. The small wards were black, their details noticeable only when the light shined directly on them. The larger wards pulsed with light as they had before.

"Does this mean we have more imps ahead?" she asked, annoyed rather than worried. Now that they knew how to deal with that particular enemy, they would be an inconvenience rather than a threat, but she would prefer to leave the prison as soon as possible.

Kut stared at the column, his brows knitted together. "How many of the corrupted did you fight before?"

"I'm not sure." She shrugged. "I'd say it was probably

under a hundred. We weren't exactly able to count at the time."

"Interesting. That's far fewer than I would have expected. It's certainly far fewer than should have been imprisoned here." The gnome raised his palm and several small light orbs winked into existence. They drifted to the column and orbited a few times before they stopped.

He approached the pillar, placed his hand on it, and murmured quietly. The wards flashed briefly.

"It's almost as if the ones you fought earlier needed energy from the others to manifest," he explained. He moved his hand away from the pillar. "This is a good thing. I hoped something like this would happen as the centuries passed and the magic of the beast weakened. They aren't destroyed, but it'll take them even longer to come back than I thought."

Hana lifted her chin and sniffed at the air. "So you're saying more won't come anytime soon? Are you sure?"

Kut nodded. "Not right away. I'm sure I can consult my uncle about the best method to secure this place. I assume the situation on Earth has changed in many ways, but if the gates are open and magic is out in the open, that makes things easier. I can't imagine anyone would want to delib-erately release such a dangerous beast."

Drysi frowned. "What about the Shadows of Rurik? Would those bastards risk it? It was a dark wizard group who released that Mountain Strider."

The gnome's eyes widened. "Are the Shadows of Rurik still around?" He sighed and shook his head as disappoint-ment suffused his face. "The misguided fools are idiotic enough to attempt something like that, perhaps, but they would not be able to control the beast. They fancied them-selves such brilliant manipulators, but there was a coarse-ness to everything they did that always drew attention to their efforts."

Hana sniffed constantly at the air and her scowl deepened.

I can understand. It smells nasty, sorry, but we're almost out of here. Suck it up a little, Hana.

"Then you'll need to be extra careful to secure this place," Alison commented. "One of the reasons we're here is because your uncle had concerns that the Shadows might be closing in on this location, both to seek power and because they had a grudge against you."

Kut clucked his tongue. "You stop one massacre and evil wizards hunt you for a millennium. They might be dangerous but they're also arrogant, which is why I bested them more often than not. We'll take special measures to keep the wards here sealed and monitor the area. If those fools dare set foot on-site, we'll know."

Hana growled. "You're wrong." Her vulpine eyes gleamed under the light of the orbs and headlamps.

"Excuse me?" He sounded genuinely insulted. "I think I understand the Shadows far better than you do, fox."

Alison turned to her friend. "Hana, what are you talking about?"

"He said there weren't any more imps." She drew her sword. "But I can smell something awful. It doesn't smell like the imps before or the death worms, but it does smell like...awful. Something's coming."

"I thought this was too easy," grumbled Alison. "Kut, a little insight?"

The gnome cut through the air with his hand. He murmured a quick incantation, and light bathed the room. It spilled into the entrance-side tunnel and revealed slowly advancing humanoid forms. A few seconds later, they broke into a run. Scratching echoed and light thuds marked their approach toward the team.

Drysi yanked out an explosive knife. "We're ready for you bastards this time. I can blow their heads off with one of these. I've barely had a chance to use them on this job."

"Whatever you do, don't damage the column," Kut shouted. "It risks disrupting all the wards, including the ones holding the beast."

"Fucking meteor beast," Drysi grumbled and tucked her knife into a sheath. She drew her wand instead. "I can still do enough with this, I suppose."

The team advanced until they stood in front of the column. They didn't have the wide space available in the other chamber but this time, they would begin the fight with knowledge of how to fell their enemy. The narrower passage in this part of the prison would also force the horde to confront the prepared Brownstone team with a small battle line. It would be a massacre.

This will be easy. It's not all that far to the exit. If we're on the surface, we won't have to hold back as much.

The monsters advanced more fully into the light.

Okay, not so simple.

Alison frowned. "What the hell?"

Instead of the gray-skinned humanoid monsters from before, a mob of running skeletons advanced on the team. Moss, fungus, and dirt covered the bones, but there wasn't any hint of skin or muscle.

"This is wrong," Kut murmured, his forehead wrinkled in confusion. "This isn't right."

"That's one way to describe it." Alison released her shadow blade and flung a shadow crescent at the neck of a skeleton. The attack sliced through the thin bone. The skull fell and the rest of the body collapsed into a pile. His brethren didn't appear to notice as they continued their forward thrust. She followed up with two rapid attacks and created two new piles. "At least they die the same way—or break the same way. Whatever."

Drysi held her wand steady as she murmured a quick incantation. The tip flashed green, and a thin eruption of energy struck the lower part of a skeleton's head. The entire bottom of the skull exploded in a shower of bone shards. What remained of the body fell with a clatter.

Mason joined the attacks with a small fireball of his own. It exploded against a skull and charred but didn't destroy it. He lowered his aim and fired another fireball, this one larger. The force of the explosion shattered the rib cage and top of the pelvis, but the aggressor didn't pull itself back together. Instead, the remnants simply toppled.

The Welsh witch grinned. "Oh, so that's how it is." She switched from her thin, focused attack to a modest fireball. The spells lacked the explosive power of one of her enchanted daggers but they also didn't knock stone and dirt loose from above.

Lily stepped back and remained close to the gnome, her magic dagger up.

Alison changed her tactics to rapid-fire explosive light bolts. One strike didn't fell a skeleton, but two turned a deadly undead threat into simply another pile of dog chew toys.

Hana sighed and sheathed her sword. "Things you can't shoot or stab are boring." She jogged over to the entrance to the previous tunnel. "Maybe I'll get lucky and they'll try to surprise us from behind."

Alison laughed. "That's not the kind of luck we need right now, but it's good to watch our backs." She pulverized another few assailants with light bolts.

The team's efforts thinned the numbers of the attacking force. The bones of their fallen crunched beneath the survivors' advance. Alison, Mason, and Drysi's constant stream of attacks had turned the tunnel into a charnel house.

When did I get to the point that huge piles of bones lying around seem almost normal?

Kut placed his hand back on the column and murmured incantations under his breath. She hoped he would manage to turn the skeleton spigot off.

"None of them have gotten up again yet," she noted. "That's a good sign." She took a few ragged breaths. Even with her high magic level, the constant stream of offensives drained her. It would have been easier if she could have concentrated magic into a bigger explosive attack. "How we doing, Kut? There are fewer of them, but they're still coming."

"This isn't right," he muttered.

"We should be good soon," Lily shouted.

I'm making her use that ability too much. If we keep this up, she'll be stuck looking into the future permanently.

Another minute passed as Alison, Mason, and Drysi

continued their stream of magical destruction, their breathing growing shallow and rapid. The final enemy suffered an attack from all three at the same time. The combined efforts blew him into dozens of smaller pieces that hurtled into the wall before they dropped onto the bone-covered floor.

Drysi wiped the sweat off her forehead and took a deep breath. "I won't lie, I hate killing dead things. It feels so redundant. Where's the satisfaction?"

Hana sauntered away from the back tunnel. "You could have at least let one through for me to cut apart. Still, skeletons are nasty, so I'm not that sad."

Mason kept his wand pointed down their desired route. "Why didn't any skeletons attack us on the way in? Is this what happens after you defeat the imps? They come back as skeletons? What's next? Will we be attacked by their crawling fingers?"

Kut lowered his hand. "No, those things don't make sense. That's what I'm saying. The imps are related to the magic flow from the beast and the meteor, none of which fed those creations. The type of magic feels different and more familiar."

Alison took a deep breath. A simple layout for the prison hadn't translated into a simple job. "I don't follow you."

"Someone else is here," the gnome declared. "Someone who isn't related to or fed by the beast."

"Damn it. It has to be the Shadows." She growled a sound of annoyance. "We took too long. Is there another way out of here?"

He shook his head. "Even if there were, given the instability of the wards, we can't leave the prison undefended. Those idiots will do something we'll all regret."

"Fine." She cracked her knuckles. "Let's go have a chat with our new friends and see if they can be reasonable."

"And if they can't?"

She glared at the tunnel. "Then they join the skeletons and imps."

CHAPTER SEVENTEEN

Whenthe group emerged from the prison entrance, a small army of thirty wizards and witches in dark hooded robes stood in a half-circle about ten yards away. Most of the magicals pointed their wands at the Brownstone team, but several others stood even farther back, their wands pointed up, and chanted in unison.

A medium-sized VTOL transport plane stood parked about a hundred feet away with no one in the cockpit that Alison could see.

Is Mr D even on the way? Did the candle actually connect to him?

If it weren't for the huge number of questionable magicals, the scene might have been beautiful. An orange-red sun hung below the peaks of the mountains far in the distance, highlighting them in lovely shades of vibrant autumn. The chill of the coming night had settled in but all the recent exercise kept her from noticing it too much.

Maybe we can talk our way out of this. Probably not, but it's worth a try. I wish this was one of those jobs where finding the place was the hardest part.

It didn't matter. The people standing in front of her needed to understand who they were threatening.

She waved. "Nice skeletons. I'm sorry we had to destroy them. It was good exercise, though." She cracked a few knuckles. "It was all atmospheric—skeletons in an ancient underground building—but it's a little early for Halloween."

A witch stepped forward and lowered her hood. The beautiful blonde woman smiled coldly, her crystal eyes piercing.

"Hello, Alison," she said in English. "I never thought I'd have to deal with you at a place like this, but life presents opportunities and it's up to us to seize them, yes?" The words were clear, but she had a noticeable Russian accent.

"No offense, but I have zero idea who you are."

"You may call me Tionna for the few short minutes you'll still be alive."

Kut sneered. "You're with the Shadows of Rurik, aren't you? I should have annihilated you eight hundred years ago. I thought your little cult of troublemakers wouldn't amount to much, but now you're here, the last place you should be."

"It is you, isn't it, gnome?" Tionna replied, her voice full of wonder. She threw her head back and laughed. "How Heaven smiles upon us. When we learned what this place might be, we wondered if you would be involved. Our history spoke of you dying to help those barbarians, but I could never be sure." She smiled, but it didn't reach her eyes. She also hadn't lowered her wand. "I never thought I would see the famous gnome with my own eyes. You've become a myth—a legend and someone who earned the enmity of the Shadows—and now, you've been delivered to us to pay for your crimes against us."

He scoffed. "You are as short-sighted as always. This is not a battle you want to fight, not for my sake, but for yours."

"Oh, you understand nothing if you believe that."

Alison sighed. "I only know a little about your group. And I know you have a bounty, but I don't care about that. Right now, I feel merciful, and I have bigger problems than a group of troublemaking magicals. I'm sure Russian bounty hunters will deal with you sooner rather than later."

Tionna sneered. "Feeble efforts throughout the centuries haven't ended the Shadows. They won't in the future, either."

"Let me be clear. If you have big designs on looting for artifacts, there are none in there." Alison nodded at the prison entrance. "It's dangerous, and it needs to remain sealed. There's nothing in there but death."

Lily stepped beside her, her eyes narrowed on the Russian witch, but she didn't say anything.

Kut pointed to the chanting group. "Those idiots are trying to disrupt the wards."

"Yes, they are," Tionna confirmed. "It'll simplify things, so we're doing it now." Her gaze flicked from the gnome to Lily. "I have little reason to doubt you, Alison, about the artifacts. The Shadows don't seek to be your enemy, but nor can we be seen to fear any woman, and we need to justify the effort put into coming here. You, of all people, must understand the importance of reputation, yes?"

Alison gritted her teeth as her frustration reached boiling point. "If you disrupt the wards, you'll not do anything but release something terrible that will kill a vast number of people, including you. Since you're probably the culprits who shot our plane down, I already have all the reasons in the world to retaliate, but I'm trying to give you a chance to not be a total idiot. I'd also rather not risk disrupting the wards more than they already have been."

This woman can't be that damned deluded, can she?

The Russian shook her wand. "We already suspected everything you're telling me. The strange wards here didn't feel like they were trying to keep someone out as much as something in. It's unfortunate. We thought this might be the tomb of Genghis Khan and contain powerful artifacts, but a destructive creature that might damage nearby countries is useful in its own way."

Oh, great. She thinks that's actually a good plan. It's time to put this in terms she can better understand.

"I'm prepared to kill you to stop that. I'm prepared to kill all of you to stop that." Alison kept her hands at her side. Summoning her blade now might start an unnecessary fight and risk further disruption of the wards. She doubted these wizards and witches would be as easy to defeat as the skeletons, but she also realized she had little hope that she could talk them out of it. "If you know anything about me, you know I'll do it. Everyone's heard about what I did to the Seventh Order."

"Do you care so much about people you don't even know?" Tionna chuckled. "You're one woman. You can't bring peace to even your own country, let alone the world. If we release whatever creature rests below, it won't harm your precious country or city."

"None of that gives you the right to kill innocent people," she retorted. "And you don't seem to understand that this could backfire on you. If you don't give a crap about them, what about your life? Are you ready to die when it emerges and eats you?"

Kut gestured toward the entrance. "You will not be able to control it, witch. We could not control it or even defeat it. In the end, we could only seal it."

Tionna shook her head, her face a mask of glee. "We won't die because you'll distract it out of your precious sense of obligation while we leave, but we're reasonable. It doesn't necessarily serve our immediate goals to release whatever strange creature is inside."

Alison allowed herself a sigh of relief. "I'm glad you've thought this through. Why don't you get on your plane and fly home?"

"We'll need something in exchange. Otherwise, this is nothing more than simple capitulation." The witch shrugged. "I think an exchange is only fair." She pointed to Kut and Lily. "Give them to us and we'll leave. That is simple, yes? Two lives for what? Hundreds? Thousands? Tens of thousands? You would know. You seem very concerned with how dangerous this creature is."

Hana growled. "You crazy bitch."

Alison threw up her arm to warn her friend off. "I was hired to bring him back, and Lily's a friend of mine. You're insane if you think I would hand them over to you. Kut, I can understand, but why the hell do you want her? Do you need a Gray Elf for some sick ritual?"

Lily gasped. "That's why she seems so familiar. Alison, this woman looks a lot like Yulia Solokova."

Her breath caught. Yulia Solokova AKA Snegurka and the Snow Maiden. The deceased ice witch had almost killed Shay several times, and she had ties to the dark fate of Lily's father.

The past can be ignored, but it always catches up with you.

The witch glared at the elf. "Oh, so you understand who I am?" She uttered a dark chuckle and her gaze flicked back to Alison. "Your mother should die, too, but the blood debt for my sister can be satisfied with only the elf's life. That gnome should already be dead anyway. It's a small sacrifice, and if you're so concerned about the creature, it shouldn't even be a difficult choice."

Kut scrubbed a hand down his face. "You idiots really need to stop trying to disrupt the wards before it's too late."

"I'll give you one last chance," Alison offered, her voice tight. "Stop the ritual, turn around, get on that plane, and leave. Otherwise, I'll do what I have to."

Tionna scoffed. "You should have taken our offer, Alison. Now, you'll all die here for nothing but a gnome who left history centuries ago and a worthless Gray Elf murderer."

Alison conjured a shadow blade in her hand and glared at the witch. "Her name is Lily and she's my friend."

"Enough of this." The Russian scoffed. "Kill them all."

CHAPTER EIGHTEEN

Alison swept her arms in front of her and shoved magic into a thin but wide shield. The witches and wizards released a barrage of fireballs, ice lances, electrical bolts, and even a mysterious lavender goo. The attacks pelted the barrier, which strained and finally collapsed.

She vaulted upward and her shadow wings came into being. The sudden movement confused the Shadows, who responded by dividing their attacks. Some fired at her, while others concentrated on the rest of her team. A few fireballs and dark orbs struck her and stung but didn't destroy her shields. She thrust her palm out and launched a light bolt at Tionna. The witch hissed as the magic exploded against her, but the shimmering shield around her held firm. She backed away while her brethren advanced with a constant stream of magical attacks.

I already miss the skeletons.

Drysi threw a dagger into one side of the enemy formation. The explosion toppled several men and women in a flurried shower of sand and smoke.

"Take that, you bastards," she shouted.

Mason charged toward the opposite side in a rapid zigzag and his enhanced speed pushed him to a near blur. His specialties might have made him less effective against skeletons but living and breathing magicals were easier to defeat due to their hearts and brains.

I gave them a chance, and they rejected it. It's all on them now.

Hana sprinted forward, her *tachi* and its wielder both ready for blood. She pounced on an enemy before the wizard could attack and her swipe forced him back. The next blow went through his shield easily, opened him from abdomen to neck, and drenched the sand with his blood. The fox moved on before he'd even fallen.

Lily squeezed off two quick rounds into the closest wizard. The man's face turned from a sneering grin to horror as her anti-magic rounds drilled through his shield and into his head. He fell back with a wide-eyed death stare and his wand spun wildly before it landed tip-first in the sand.

Despite the Brownstone team carving into the Shadows of Rurik, none of the men or women turned to flee. Determination settled onto their faces. They were brave for people about to die.

Alison couldn't find respect for them. They might not be physical cowards, but they were willing to sacrifice others. That made them a different kind of coward. Much worse cowards, by her standards.

Kut knelt, placed his hand on the ground, and murmured softly. She wondered for a moment what he might be doing, but a sizzling mass of lavender goo pelted her shield and drained it far more quickly than she expected. She turned in the air to avoid the follow-up attack with the odd substance.

You do what you need to do, Kut, and we'll do what we need to do.

She might not know the gnome well, but if he had any interest in freeing the beast, despite his disclaimers, it would have made more sense to do it inside when he had direct access to some of the wards.

Alison spun and changed direction. She layered another shield over herself before she strafed the Shadows with a combination of quick-fire light bolts and shadow crescents. The magicals' shields were strong enough to not fail after a single strike, but the wizards and witches staggered under the onslaught and grimaced in pain. She frowned. The men performing the ritual hadn't stopped.

It's time to make them pay attention to me.

She turned toward them and prepared to throw a few spells. A huge wall of sand surged up and she impacted with it, the packed grains as hard as rock. She floated backward and shook her head to clear it. Without her shields, she might have broken her neck.

A witch on the ground gestured with her wand, and the sand wall fragmented and swarmed the Drow like a cloud of the two worlds' angriest gnats. She flung off a few attacks, but without clear visibility, she couldn't risk a major offensive that might harm her friends.

"Nice trick," she muttered.

Most fights were too fast-paced for many complicated spells, but when someone had dozens of allies, they could get away with attacks that were harder to counter.

Alison poured shadow magic into her palms and stretched her arms out. She channeled energy for several seconds before she released it in an explosive wave in all directions. The spell drove the sand cloud away from her.

She dropped immediately to divebomb the witch and two of her light bolts staggered the woman. A shadow crescent depleted the Shadow's defenses, and another light bolt catapulted her away, her chest blackened and charred.

You had a good idea, I'll give you that. Too bad you're helping to do something psychotic.

Hana swept through the far flank and swung and sliced with a rhythm that was almost a dance. A few shields, including a wizard using rotating hardened sand, held better than others, but none of her targets could take more than a handful of blows from the *tachi*. Mason disrupted counterattacks by advancing from the other side. His punches and kicks launched victims directly into the deadly nine-tailed fox's path and she didn't hesitate to cut them down.

Lily's gun went dry. She tucked it into her pocket and darted forward, not as fast as Hana or Mason but still dodged every direct attack with ease. One wizard growled in frustration and aimed his wand for a point-blank shot on the apparently unarmed woman. She whipped her magic dagger out and sliced his throat before he could utter the first syllable of his spell. He fell and clutched his neck as he gurgled and spat blood.

Alison, suspended above the fighting, spun toward the ritual team. Despite the bloody battle below, the Shadows of Rurik were a minor inconvenience by themselves. Whatever bizarre, ridiculous creature they might free was the true problem. She didn't want to have to call her Dad for help because a giant magical alien monster rampaged through Mongolia and China.

How many of these things are hidden underground somewhere? There has been any number of meteor and comet strikes throughout the years.

She shook her head and reminded herself that she didn't have time to worry about problems in the future. The priority was to stop the immediate threat.

A grinning Drysi ended the ritual with the help of several explosive daggers thrown in rapid succession. The shields of the wizards conducting the chant failed after the first explosion, but they managed to remain standing. A second strike scattered them. The third scorched them, and the fourth sent them to their rewards in the afterlife.

Flying low, Alison circled the blood-splattered sandy battlefield. The wizards and witches of the Shadows of Rurik lay on the ground with various injuries, all dead or dying. Only one opponent remained. Tionna held a spear of pure fire in her glowing left hand. Her wand was trained on Lily who stood a few yards away.

Alison could end the fight with a few quick attacks, but given the opponent, this was something Lily needed to handle.

Kut remained on one knee, his eyes closed, and continued to murmur quietly.

I don't know if that's a good thing or a bad thing. Maybe he's merely praying at this point.

"Was it worth it, Tionna?" Lily asked and swept her free hand in a grand gesture. "Shooting the plane down. All of this?"

The witch laughed. "This doesn't end with me. You'll die, you elf bitch, and I will strike at Alison from beyond the grave. The Shadows of Rurik have been weakened and bloodied, but as long as there is one of us left, you'll never be safe."

Hana scoffed. She shook the blood off her blade before she sheathed it. "You'll strike at her from beyond the grave. Do you plan to come back as a skeleton? Please. Those were easy to destroy." She rolled her eyes. "You were easy to defeat. The Seventh Order was tougher than you."

"Alison Brownstone has so many enemies." Tionna kept her focus on Lily. "Things have been set in motion, and you will suffer the vengeance of the Shadows of Rurik."

Mason pounded his fist into his palm with a loud thud. "You've heard of what happens to people who target Brownstone Security." He glowered at the witch. "Ask the Seventh Order, or what's left of them. You've lost."

"I don't care." She snarled her fury. "Her mother and her Gray Elf friend murdered my sister. I'll sacrifice every Shadow if that is what it takes to get my revenge."

"Your sister was a sociopathic killer," Lily yelled in response. "If she didn't want to be killed, all she had to do was leave Shay and me alone."

The Russian's angry visage shifted and a pleasant, blissful smile settled over her face. "It doesn't matter now." She drew her spear back. "You'll be dead soon enough."

Lily whipped her left arm up while her right hand remained in her pocket. Her dagger streaked toward its target. It bounced off the witch's shield, which was barely a shimmer.

"Pathetic," Tionna declared. "I expected more from you."

The Gray Elf removed her right hand from her pocket with her gun in hand. She pulled the trigger three times.

Tionna jerked and stumbled. Blood blossomed from the three bullet holes. Her fire spear vanished, and her wand fell at her feet. The witch collapsed to her knees and coughed blood.

"All those attacks depleted my artifact," Lily explained. She tucked her gun into her holster. "And I needed to load a new mag. I could have let someone else kill you, but we both know I needed to be the one to do it."

"Damn that Wood Elf for leading me to you." The wounded witch coughed a few more times. "I know she wasn't who she appeared, but now…" She uttered a final pained chuckle before she sagged and her chest stopped moving.

Alison landed and released the magic fueling her wings. "Wood Elf?"

Lily shrugged. "I've made a few enemies on the job, but I honestly don't remember running into any Wood Elves I've pissed off. You don't see many of them in my line of work."

She's like me. I thought I was done with Scott until that woman messed with me at the resort. There's always someone—a relative or an apprentice. Dad barely hunts anymore, and he still runs into trouble.

"It doesn't matter now," she declared and shook her head.

"You're not worried about all that vengeance talk?" Lily

asked. "If she was psycho enough to set all this up, it might not all be empty threats."

"She'll need to get in line for both of us." Alison pointed to the transport in the distance. "No one can fly that thing, but at least we'll have a working radio. I don't see Mr D anywhere, so even if the candle somehow did connect with him, he can't portal here."

Drysi stepped over a dead wizard and pointed at Kut. "What's he doing?" She frowned and her hands twitched. "He did it through the whole damned fight. Do you feel that?"

The Drow frowned and nodded. Now that she was no longer focused on the battle, she sensed that the magical pressure in the area was considerably higher than it had been before.

That can't be good.

They all turned toward the gnome. Mason moved in front of Alison. Kut continued his murmured chanting for about ten seconds before he stood and dusted the sand off his knees.

"There is a problem," he announced. "Unfortunately."

Hana groaned. "The meteor monster is coming?"

He shook his head. "No. I was able to stabilize the wards despite their efforts, and you killed them before they could defeat my efforts."

Everyone sighed with relief.

"Unfortunately, to do that," he continued, "I had to reroute some magical flows so some of that excess magic will need to be vented. That is the problem. It will be…destructive."

"Vented?" Alison raised an eyebrow. "Destructive? In what way?"

"The energy will come out as a huge magical explosion centered right here." Kut pushed his hands together and mimed a blast with his hands. "Don't worry. It won't disrupt the wards on the prison, but it will cause considerable damage on the surface. Anything not protected will most likely be destroyed. And we have very little time—maybe less than a minute and two at most."

"We should run, A," Mason suggested.

The pressure continued to build and violent tremors shook the sand.

"We don't have time." Alison pointed to Kut. "Everyone, gather around him. We'll stack our shields as best we can. It's our only chance. If we fail, we'll be too dead to care."

The gnome offered her a merry smile and raised his hands. A glowing dome appeared and surrounded the Brownstone team. Alison lifted her arms and channeled her magic into an interior shield inside his. Mason and Drysi raised their wands and began to chant. The overlapping distortions of the shields blocked the outside. It was if they looked through frosted glass. The potent magical pressure all around them continued to grow, along with the intensity of the tremors.

Hana huffed. "If I get blown up after all that, I'll be really pissed." She wrinkled her nose. "I think it's coming. Lily, what do you see?"

She shook her head. "I'd rather not check. Sometimes, you don't want to see the trap coming."

Alison's stomach lurched. The tremors might be

wreaking havoc, but the overwhelming magical pressure was the real source of her struggle.

Exactly how much power is he venting? How big will this explosion be?

Her jaw tightened, and she continued to shove magic into her shield. All her little complaints might not matter soon if she was reduced to a pile of ash.

"Come on," she muttered. "We can do this."

A bright flash surrounded them. The huge magical eruption struck their nested shields. Blinded, Alison hissed as the wave pounded through their barrier and flung them away from their makeshift joint magical fortress.

She impacted with the sand and groaned as her vision cleared and she rolled onto her side. The blast had left a massive crater and the displaced sand filled the sky in a massive mushroom cloud. The top of the prison was visible, but it appeared untouched despite the destruction.

After a moment to catch her breath, she stood and rubbed her sore jaw absently. Sand drifted down like coarse rain. A few drops of blood dripped from a cut on her forehead, but a small touch of shadow magic sealed the scrape. Burn holes covered her clothes.

A prone Mason pushed himself up several yards away. His clothes were in no better shape than hers, but he wasn't dead. That was a plus.

"Are you okay, A?"

"I'm fine. Drysi? Hana? Lily?"

The Welsh witch yanked her half-buried arm out of the sand. A jagged cut across her cheek seeped blood, and her jacket was blackened and one of the sleeves burned away, and the skin beneath was a dull red. Considering the scale of the explosion, their minor injuries were almost miraculous.

Hana and Lily both sat up only a few yards apart. They were in better shape than everyone else.

"Kut?" Alison turned slowly in a circle in search of the gnome. She found him standing right behind her, his suit apparently untouched.

He stared at her, newfound appreciation in his eyes. "If it were only me trying to block that, I would have died. You and your team are very impressive."

"I'm glad you approve." She smiled, surveyed the area, and brushed residual sand off her face. Other than a few charred bones protruding, there was little left of the bodies. A loud groan erupted from her, however, when her gaze settled on the plane in the distance. It was a burning wreck of twisted metal.

Kut followed her gaze. "Don't worry. Now that no one's trying to kill us, I can use the link my uncle attempted to establish with the candle to communicate with him. It's over. We've won."

Alison shook her head and studied the crater. "It did end with something blowing up, after all."

Hana gave her a thumb's up. "Only the desert."

CHAPTER NINETEEN

With a sigh, Alison shifted the phone in her hand where she reclined on the comfortable sofa in her hotel room. Mr D had arrived with a plane to recover them, and she'd wondered how Tahir was faring. Now, she knew. There was trouble on both sides of the world.

"You're kidding me," she muttered. "Someone's been skulking around the building. That might be what that damned witch was talking about when she talked about revenge. They must have an assassin waiting for me when I come back."

Their return to Ulaanbaatar meant access to a normal phone grid. She hadn't even brought her phone with her on the job, concerned about its potential destruction, and had assumed the satellite phone would be enough.

Tahir snorted. "We're rotating shifts, and Sonya's so full of adrenaline and energy potions, I don't think she could go to sleep even if she wanted to. If the person she detected is a member of the Shadows of Rurik, they should have taken their chance when it was still nighttime here. If they're waiting for you, they're waiting to die."

"They might not be waiting for me," she insisted. "If you need to, bring all hands on deck. If you need to call AET, do it."

"Don't worry, Alison." He sounded amused. "Your building will still be here when you get back. A single wizard is hardly a concern."

"I don't care about the building."

"It's fine, Alison," he replied, his tone friendly. "You're not fighting alone, either there or here. Even without you in Seattle, we have highly trained employees with access to anti-magic gear, along with a witch and a wizard—and a rather intelligent wizard at that. If worse comes to worst, I'll lie to Omni and tell him the attackers hurt Hana."

Alison grimaced. If Tahir did that, her building probably wouldn't be there. Woe to any man who got between Omni and his mommy.

"Fine." She capitulated, exasperated and her neck tight with worry. "Do what you need to do but be safe. The next flight is not until tomorrow morning, so we'll be home—Wait." She snapped her fingers. "Mr D can probably open a portal for us. Oh, wait. Maybe he can't. He made us fly here, and he sent a plane to pick us up. I'll let you know if I can come back sooner. Talk to you later."

"We'll be fine. Talk to you soon." Tahir ended the call.

She curled her hand into a fist and reminded herself once again that she needed to improve her portal magic. Although she was close, it wasn't good enough. She needed to be able to return to Seattle instantly. Even if they boarded a supersonic flight that minute, it'd still take them too many hours to return. Could the gnome not actually portal, or was there something else going on?

They'd worried about taking a flight to the capital, but Mr D assured them he would account for that and he had in the form of a rather powerful shielding artifact he'd sent along with the rescue plane. There were no other attacks, but she was dubious that the Shadows of Rurik only had a few dozen members.

Maybe he can portal and maybe he can't. I'll find out in twenty minutes.

Alison stepped out of the steamy shower and slipped a robe on. Her magic might have healed her wounds, but that didn't change the fact that it had been a long day and Brownstone Security might be attacked at any minute. She wanted to believe that the Shadows of Rurik were defeated, but a final desperate suicide attack could still hurt too many people. Her instincts insisted that she needed to be there to protect her friends.

There was a light knock on her door and she frowned. Mr D was early.

When she opened the door, the tuxedo-clad gnome stood on the other side with a broad smile.

She stepped back and gestured inside. "I wasn't quite ready yet, but before we begin, I have a question."

He entered the room and closed the door behind him. "What is it?"

"Can you portal us directly to Seattle?" she asked.

"Yes, although to do that, you'll need to wait a week.

Unless you're looking forward to sightseeing in Mongolia, it'd be more efficient for you to simply fly home."

"A week?" She folded her arms. "Why a week?"

"The magic involved in using the candle extracts a cost," he explained. "But it was necessary to recover my nephew. It's fortunate that despite some of my miscalculations, he was still able to make use of the connection." He headed over to the sofa and sat on the edge. "I'm sorry, Miss Brownstone. Both Kut and I have paid a price for this incident, and it'll take us both time to fully recover."

Alison sighed. "Well, it was worth a shot." She frowned. "The Shadows didn't arrive simply because they tracked us there. One of them mentioned a Wood Elf who helped them. Do you know anything about that?"

Mr D furrowed his brow and his gaze lowered. He shook his head. "I don't know of any Wood Elf who might help them. At least you can claim their bounties."

"That'll be a little complicated since there wasn't anything left." She shrugged. "Not everyone's willing to accept the truth, but I'm not worried about a few evil wizards and witches being gone from the world even if I don't get paid for it."

He inclined his head. "Family is important to gnomes, and you've done me a great service. Kut is also grateful, even though the ordeal has left him exhausted. Coming out of that spell like he did was far more taxing than he let on. He's always been too stoic for his own good."

"And the beast?"

"I've already spoken with contacts in the Chinese and Mongolian governments," the gnome explained. "Kut and I will aid them in initial efforts while they look into a longer-term solution. They'll also contact the Indians, Russians, and Americans for additional magical aid. Don't worry, Miss Brownstone. This is one time where everyone understands the risk, and they will do what is necessary to handle it. You've performed admirably, but we can take it from here. Again, thank you for your assistance in this matter."

"You're welcome."

"I apologize for being unable to open a portal for you." He stood. "But I have contacts who can provide a similar service. It will probably take me a few hours to get hold of them. Would that suffice? Consider it a bonus."

She smiled, immediately relieved. "Thanks, Mr D. I'd appreciate it."

CHAPTER TWENTY

Sonya's gaze darted constantly as she sought any hint of an enemy on her drone and camera feeds. She hadn't slept all night, but with a fresh energy potion in her, it wouldn't matter. Alison and the rest of the magical team would portal back from Mongolia soon. All they had to do was hold out until then. Once the Dark Princess returned, the jerks would pay for daring to sniff around her building.

"Shouldn't we be on lockdown or something?" she asked and turned to face Tahir. "At least until Alison gets back?"

Her mentor sat at his own workstation, his expression more bored than uneasy. He had a few feeds up, but he seemed to be going through news articles.

He might be better at automated things than me, but he's not taking this seriously. That's not cool, man. Not cool.

Tahir shook his head. "A vague threat from a dying witch isn't the same thing as a major invasion. Brownstone Security has a reputation. We can't damage that by jumping at every shadow."

"This isn't a shadow. It's a guy hiding." She gestured toward her screens. "And we lost the guy I saw earlier. He could be anywhere and could have a bomb, or he could be set up with a sniper rifle somewhere. Maybe he's even a spotter for artillery exactly like the movie I saw the other day. A terrorist totally blows up the police station with artillery they have on the deck on an oil tanker."

The infomancer smirked. "That would be as impressive as it sounds outlandish. No, I suspect something far feebler than that. From what Alison described, these wizards were only of middling combat ability. I'm sure Jerry's team would cut through them with ease if they were appropriately equipped. Besides, attacking us so soon after a failed assault on Alison would be a mistake. We're on greater alert than normal."

"Not alert enough." She entered a few commands to increase the search radius of her linked drones. It wasn't sufficient to simply look for people as there were many on the street, either on the way to work or the local coffee shops or restaurants for a quick morning bite. The key was finding someone who was hiding.

"You'll die young if you worry so much," Tahir insisted.

Sonya rolled her eyes. "You're the one who told me forewarned is forearmed."

"Yes, but you need to worry about legitimate threats, not minor threats." He shrugged.

"You sound more like Hana each day," she mumbled. "We need to protect our people. Alison can kick ass, but she can't bring people back from the dead."

"You're correct on both accounts." He yawned and patted his mouth. "I should have used an energy potion, too. I honestly thought our little friend would have tried something by now."

"He'll do something soon." She glared at her screen. "I know he will. It's only a matter of waiting."

A shrill alarm shrieked from Sonya's computer. Her heart rate kicked up and she tapped on the relevant window to switch to a drone thermographic feed. She pointed a shaking finger at the screen.

"Do you see that?" she shouted. "I knew it. He's back!"

Tahir sighed and shook his head. "Calm down." He rolled his chair beside her and leaned closer to the screen. "And what do we have?"

Multiple red-orange heat blobs highlighted people on the street on the display.

She pointed to one. "That's Ava. She just left the building and is going somewhere."

"You don't know where she's going?"

The teenager shrugged. "I set up tracking on everyone's phones. I was cross-referencing movement, but only if they left the building." She nibbled on her lip. "I think she's going to that stupid coffee shop to get a cup of tea. She should simply pay someone to open a tea shop near here." She pointed to another heat blob a few feet behind Ava. "And look what happens when I switch to normal feed." She clicked her mouse. The sharply dressed administrative assistant remained on the feed, but there was no one following as there had been on the thermal feed.

"Interesting." Tahir smiled. "Good job."

Sonya swallowed. "We need to scramble a squad with anti-magic rounds and deflectors."

He chuckled. "If our friend was following Sienna, maybe that would be necessary. But Ava? She would find it insulting." He cleared his throat and pushed away from her workstation to roll back to his own where he tapped a quick command into his keyboard and waited. "Ava, can you hear me?" He listened a moment and nodded. "Our invisible magical from earlier is following you. Yes. Yes. Are you sure? Understood. Enjoy your tea."

His trainee stared at him and waited for an explanation with her arms folded.

"She'll handle it," he explained with a wave of his hand. "She'll also ensure there's no collateral damage, contact the police afterward, and deal with the relevant paperwork. She specifically doesn't want reinforcements and she says she needs the exercise."

"But she's not even a magical," she complained.

"You've seen what she can do," he countered. "She could probably kill both of us before we knew we were under attack."

The girl shook her fists in frustration. "I've seen her kick ass when she has a massive gun loaded with anti-magic ammo, man. Not when she walked down the street to get tea. I know she's the world's most killer administrative assistant, but she can't see invisible people."

Tahir's eyes narrowed. "Do you trust me, Sonya? Do you trust Ava?"

She looked down. "I don't want anyone to get hurt. I get nervous when everyone's really far away."

He nodded, his expression sympathetic. "I understand,

and someone will get hurt. It merely won't be one of the Brownstone team."

———

Ava tucked her phone in her purse and continued down the sidewalk. Her heels clicked against the hard surface and she maneuvered through a few stray puddles. The light rain of the last few days didn't demand an umbrella, but it had left its touch. Some people found Seattle dreary, but a good rainfall was relaxing.

She stopped and waited at an intersection for the signal to change before she strolled across. Her tea would have to wait for a few minutes until she had dealt with the present unpleasantness. Too many innocent people would be in the coffee shop, especially since so many were getting tea or coffee before heading off to work. She would deal with her rude stalker soon, but she couldn't take the chance that he had some kind of dead man's self-destruct spell.

It'd be like Morocco all over again. I'm even getting tea at a coffee shop. It's like the saying—the first time is tragedy but the second time is farce.

Applying the quote to herself might seem arrogant but she didn't care. It was appropriate, and there was never shame in accepting the truth.

Ava strolled into a narrow alley and consciously made no effort to look behind her. Her stalker needed to believe she was taking a shortcut and unaware of their presence. If he were a competent assassin, he would have spent time establishing her habits, but from what Miss Brownstone had related to Tahir, he was simply another foolish wizard who mistook his magical ability—a mere tool—as a sign of true power.

Deliberately, she stepped in a puddle and stumbled. She recovered and feigned looking at her watch. "I'll be late," she muttered and stepped out of the water. When she twisted her foot a particular way, her heel snapped off, exactly as she'd planned. She stepped out of her other shoe. "Oh, my. This is concerning."

A trained assassin always struck when they thought their target was otherwise distracted and emotionally involved in something else. The more opportunities she gave her stalker, the more she would push his hand. She listened for footsteps or any other sign of attack.

A light chuckle sounded from behind her.

She turned quickly but no one was there.

You're a fool. If you'd tried to kill me right away, you might have had some small chance. Now, you're nothing more than an inconvenience before my morning tea.

"Is someone there?" She slid her hand into her purse and injected a false tremor into her voice. "I have a Taser. You'd better leave me alone." She fought against normal discipline to feign a slight trembling in her visible hand. The wolf needed to believe she was a sheep.

A louder laugh responded, definitely masculine. This time, it sounded like he was above her.

He's smart enough to not give away his position but not smart enough to not taunt me. It doesn't matter if he has magic or not. He's merely another amateur in the end. Disappointing. I thought this might actually be useful practice.

"It's your misfortune," her invisible stalker stated with a clear Russian accent. That didn't eliminate the chance that he was someone else, but it did strongly support the assumption that he was a member of the Shadows of Rurik.

"Who are you?"

"You work for Alison Brownstone. This is nothing personal, but she needs to understand what happens to those who oppose us. She can't protect people all the time."

Ava's gaze lowered to a nearby puddle. The water was displaced in two places in the shallow pool. The oversight was sloppy. The man had gone to the trouble to redirect his voice and turn invisible, but he didn't bother to take the environment into account.

She dropped her fake trembling act and her expression turned to steel. "Miss Brownstone is more merciful than me. To honor her, I'll give you a chance to turn and leave before I kill you."

The wizard laughed. He obviously thought that she still had no idea where he was. "With your Taser? I don't think you know who you're dealing with, woman."

Her hand tightened around the gun in her purse and she yanked it out and pointed it directly at him.

Let me give you this one last chance to think this through.

"Do you have any last words, woman, before you die?" the wizard asked. "Do you think your little gun will be able to stop me? You don't even know where I am."

In reply, she fired three times into his chest and he screamed. His body slowly materialized as he collapsed into the puddle, blood draining from his chest into the water. He lifted his wand, his eyes wide.

"I hold to the assumption that anyone who might target me on the street and who is worth shooting is a magical and equip myself accordingly. Non-magicals I can handle without the gun." She marched over to him. "Unfortunately, I can't let you heal and I can't ignore the possibility that you were prepared to kill me. I'm more annoyed than offended, but had it been one of the other administrative assistants, they wouldn't have been able to defend themselves." She pointed at his head and pulled the trigger.

Ava put her gun away and pulled her phone out to call the police. She looked at her skirt.

Should I ask Miss Brownstone to take care of it or should I simply have it dry cleaned?

CHAPTER TWENTY-ONE

Alison placed Mason's quiche on the table before setting her own plate down. She hadn't been sure about using Oriceran herbs, but the hearty aroma prompted her stomach to rumble.

I remember when my cooking was a biohazard, but I've become fairly damned good and I don't even need to use any magic. I'm no dining hall pixie, but I do all right.

Judging by the huge smile on Mason's face, he agreed. Or maybe he wanted to make sure he got some that night.

She sat and picked her fork up. After everything that had happened in the last week, the pure normalcy of a simple meal with her husband at home felt almost bizarre. At least a few assassins should have appeared, or maybe a toaster golem to threaten her during the cooking process.

No wonder Dad and Mom retired young. This kind of lifestyle can really wear you down. I don't think I would have been able to find someone if he wasn't already a bodyguard wizard.

A week had passed since their return from Mongolia.

Sonya and Tahir continued to monitor the area around the Brownstone Security building, both magically and technologically, along with chatter on the net. There'd been no hint of a follow-up attack or reconnaissance attempts. Alison's informants and contacts suggested that despite Tionna's threats, the Shadows of Rurik had been effectively destroyed, the failed assassin one of the few remaining members. Unlike the Seventh Order, they'd never been a large group. No one had turned up any useful information on who might have pointed the Shadows at Lily and her.

Tionna and the others must have estimated that they would take far fewer casualties. It didn't matter. Even if there were dozens of other members hidden somewhere, none seemed eager to face Alison Brownstone or even her administrative assistant.

Lily intended to visit Alison's parents' to chat with Shay about the vengeful witch and her sister. That was one part of both their pasts that Alison hadn't shared and she wasn't jealous about that. The fewer psychotic magicals hunting her, the better.

She took a mouthful of the quiche and savored the strong, herbaceous notes. "Damn, I'm good."

"It tastes great, A," Mason agreed with a smile. He speared his quiche, pulled another mouthful out, and waved it on his fork like a trophy. "I was skeptical when you mentioned the Oriceran herbs, but it's worked out well. Some of them are crazy. It's hard to know with so many different palates on one planet. After all, it's not like every human agrees about what tastes good."

She nodded and knew all too well that she had to take into account the source of the herbs.

I'll never listen to a dwarf again about what's supposed to be delicious.

"I decided if Dad can risk experimenting with his precious barbecue, I can be a little more adventurous with my cooking." She chuckled. "I don't want to somehow be more stuck in my ways than D—"

Her phone came to life. The ring tone was the main theme from *Swan Lake* and her heart immediately raced.

It doesn't have to mean anything. Maybe she simply wants to say hi.

Mason shook his head. "You don't have to take that."

She pulled the phone out of her pocket. "It's Rasila."

He frowned. "Just because she and Miar have become really competitive over mini-golf doesn't mean you have to jump when they call. Sometimes, friends need a little distance."

Friends? It sounded right when he said it. That had never been their intent. They'd gone from competitors to allies to something more, even though the succession remained a tangled knot that would likely require blood to unravel.

"Rasila never calls for that kind of thing. If she tries to reach me, it has to be important." She tapped the phone to accept the call. "Hello?"

"We need to discuss some matters," Rasila replied, her tone pleasant even though her words were curt. "And we must discuss them tonight. As certain types of subterfuge are no longer necessary, I will come directly to your house. It's far more secure than most places we meet."

"Huh? You're coming here?"

Mason muttered something under his breath.

"Yes," Rasila replied. "I'll be there in one hour and I wish to speak to you without the humans present. I don't care if you tell them later, but there's a certain pride I find myself still attached to. At some point, if you become queen, I'll learn to deal with it." She ended the call.

Alison stood with a sigh. "You and Sonya will need to take a little trip for a couple of hours. I'm sorry, but something has her spooked."

"What's going on?" Mason asked.

"I don't know yet, but Rasila wants to meet on short notice, and she wants to meet me here. That tells me she's worried about something that'll happen that's both annoying and coming soon." She hurried toward the living room. "Even if she shows up as Ruby, it means she's trying to send a signal to anyone in the know who might be watching. If she's willing to go that far, it has to be Drow crap."

"And what signal is that?" he called from the dining room. He stood and pushed his chair under the table.

"That she's not merely someone helping me in the shadows. She's my ally."

On the edge of the couch, Rasila crossed her legs and settled her hands in her lap. She had entered in her dark-haired human guise, but as soon as her host closed the door, the other Drow reverted to her natural dark-skinned, white-haired form. Both were beautiful and striking in their own ways.

Alison folded her arms and stood behind Mason's favorite recliner. "Okay, I was in the middle of dinner with Mason and you ruined it. I kicked my own husband out of his house because you're still getting used to him being human. I assume you have a good reason."

Rasila smirked. "I can't believe you married a human."

"You seem to keep forgetting I'm half-human."

The other woman shook her head lightly. "Yes, I do, and I'll admit he seems to be a good warrior. If he's earned your respect, I should not question you. If I'd been raised on Earth, I might find such a man appealing." She tilted her head and considered the thought.

"Please tell me you didn't come here to bitch about my marriage." She pinched the bridge of her nose, then pointed to the door. "If that's the case, there's the door. I don't require your approval for my relationship."

"You're right on both counts. We have more important matters to discuss." Rasila uncrossed her legs and the small amount of lingering amusement vanished from her face. She leaned forward with a frown. "I came across some information earlier today that I thought was relevant and potentially time-sensitive. I know you've been seeking information about the Shadows of Rurik and any Wood Elves who are allied with them or even any who have bragged about aiding them for money."

Alison nodded. "I have. I didn't really think to ask you. That didn't seem like your area. Sorry."

Rasila straightened and scoffed, her forehead wrinkled in frustration. "You forget that I have no problem taking advantage of resources on Earth. Just because Drow are superior doesn't mean there aren't useful tools and allies among the races of this planet. But no matter. The issue isn't my relationship with the magical underworld or even how I found this information. The issue is what I found about Mongolia and how it pertains to both of us."

"Both of us? Huh? What do you have to do with what happened in Mongolia? The Shadows were obsessed with killing a gnome, my friend, and me because of a personal incident in the past. None of it was Drow-specific."

Alison wasn't surprised the woman knew about Mongolia, even if she hadn't specified to her other informants that she was interested in the Shadows of Rurik because of the attack that took place there. The involvement of so many countries in containing the beast led to news leaking about something unusual in the Mongolian desert. For some reason, the media had latched onto the idea that a North Korean strategic magic experiment had gone awry, and various countries were working to clean it up. Oddly enough, the North Korean government pointedly didn't publicly deny the accusation. She assumed the Chinese offered them something to take the blame while the other countries worked to clean up the meteor mess.

All these countries working together. Is it possible that all we need for world unity is strange alien magical monsters threatening us?

"First, let me verify my facts," Rasila replied. "That will help me be sure about what I'm about to tell you. You traveled to the Gobi Desert. There, you were attacked by the Shadows of Rurik. I assume you butchered them like the weak cattle they are and interrogated one before he admitted a Wood Elf sent them to you? And that is why you've asked about him?"

"That's a little more colorful than how I would have described it, and it's not totally accurate, but that's the basic gist."

"The Wood Elf connection is what fascinated me," her companion explained. "There are twisted Wood Elves out there, but one bold enough to strike at an ally of Alison Brownstone would be a rare creature. Unfortunately, the story of what I found isn't so simple, especially since some of this information came to me through one of my servants. She informed me about a Wood Elf interested in collecting magical enhancement artifacts from a tomb raider in Krakow. This only came to my attention because I was interested in acquiring some of these artifacts as well. One needs to know who is interfering with one's ambitions."

Alison chuckled. "So it's less that you were helping me and more that someone crossed you, and since they happen to have annoyed me too, you assume we should get together to deal with them?"

"A convergence of opportunities isn't a bad thing, Alison. In this case, it's given me insight, because one of my people observed something curious." Rasila narrowed her eyes. "And that has me worried."

"What did they see? The Wood Elf had two-for-one artifact coupons?"

"No. She saw one using Drow-style shadow magic. She was insistent on that point."

"It wasn't a Wood Elf?" Alison frowned. "It was a shapeshifted Drow?"

"That's the most likely explanation." Rasila's form shimmered and settled into a perfect replica of Hana in a bright yellow crop top and too-tight jeans. She smirked and reverted to her true appearance. "That's your one weakness—having to actually use a spell to change your appearance."

When did she even see Hana in that outfit? Or does she simply have that much of a feel for her personality?

"Okay, a Drow faked being a Wood Elf and pointed the Shadows of Rurik at Lily." She thought it over for a few seconds and hissed in irritation. "No, Lily was only the bait. If she had a Drow enemy, I would know about it and she would know about it. This was about pointing the Shadows at me using Lily. The only question is who is behind it at all."

She already knew the answer to the question, but she wanted to hear someone else say it aloud. The implications would ruin her week, no matter how many delicious quiches she made.

"The individual Drow could have been anyone," Rasila suggested, "but this kind of maneuvering is beneath someone as straightforward and arrogant as Novati. Not only that, the timing so close to the last time Drae offered her deal passes beyond the suspicious to the obvious. It has to be her." She scowled. "It's disgusting. I don't mind subterfuge, but this plan didn't end with her challenging you directly. She's gone too far. Even the mere attempt means she's ready for much more."

Alison groaned. "I half-hoped you'd say it was simply a disgruntled loser who hated me for being half-human."

"If only, although that often describes Drae." The other

Drow's scowl bled into a hungry smile. "The time has come, it seems. Things are now about to get interesting."

"Bloody, you mean."

"As I said, interesting."

"I can't have other people dragged into Drow politics." She thumped her fist on the table. "Damn it. I'd handle her directly, but I'm not sure if it'll cause a big mess. Maybe I should go to the Guardians and lodge some kind of complaint."

Rasila wrinkled her nose in disgust and scoffed. "The Guardians are useless. You should keep in mind they have not made any real efforts to address the succession crisis, even with Miar expressing interest in supporting them. They are hoping we weaken one another so they'll be able to secure their hold on power. If they were bolder, I could at least admire that, but it's hard to look at their actions as anything other than rank cowardice."

"They're not the bad guys. They helped apprehend Laena and kept things stable. There wasn't some bloody purge after. I don't want to formally support them only because I think my situation is more complicated."

Rasila barked out a laugh. "Sometimes I forget that despite all your power and loyalty, you can be blindingly naïve. Even if most were not part of her true inner circle, many of the Guardians served Laena loyally until your father defeated her." Her nostrils flared. "Don't make the mistake of thinking of them as plucky revolutionaries in tri-corner hats angered about excessive taxes on tea. They are cowardly opportunists who could have deposed the queen before without relying on an outsider to help them. They are like all those in authority who seize it by relying on others. They care about nothing but preserving their own power."

Alison blinked, surprised at the woman's ability to draw on low-level American iconography with ease. She constantly underestimated her based on some of her dealings with other Drow.

"I'm not sure about that," she responded, "and I understand where you're coming from, but I can't leave this alone."

"I'm not suggesting you should, but we also need to take into account that Novati is poised for action. That's the other thing I wanted to bring to your attention. The Guardians have quietly recruited loyalists to bolster their forces. With this latest action by Drae, things are on the cusp. I doubt we have months and years to find answers."

"We can't be sure it's Drae," Alison pointed out. "That's the only thing I'm worried about. Killing someone based on circumstantial evidence isn't my style."

"It's almost certainly her. Everything about it smells of her." Rasila sneered. "The civil war is imminent, Alison. Everyone senses it, and everyone but you is prepared for it. Many non-Drow have quietly left Drow territory during the last month. King Oriceran has Light Elf and other allied armies on alleged training maneuvers near Drow territory. It's not unprecedented, but it's also convenient timing."

Bile rose in the back of Alison's force. "Wait? Are you saying they'll invade?"

Rasila shook her head. "Fortunately, I doubt they will. Say what you will for the Light Elves and their arrogance, they love the Great Treaty more than most. They are there only if things get out of hand and threaten people beyond Drow borders. If no magic forbidden by the Great Treaty is used and Drow stick to killing other Drow, they'll be content to let us continue the slaughter because the alternative is the spread of the war into other areas."

Damn it. Why couldn't you have all found solutions to this years ago?

Alison's phone came alive with another familiar ring tone. This time, it was Ava's.

"I need to take this," she explained. "Ava's working late at the office, and I need to make sure the Shadows aren't trying anything—or with my luck, Drae."

Rasila nodded. "Go ahead."

"Hello, Ava."

"Miss Brownstone," her assistant replied. "I apologize for disturbing you in the evening, but an unusual guest has arrived, and I think this will require your personal attention."

Alison sighed. "Another invisible wizard assassin?"

"That would be preferable," Ava explained and faint annoyance flavored her words. "There is a Drow here who insists on speaking to you. He refuses to identify himself to a mere human such as myself."

"A Drow? Is he threatening anyone there?" She clenched her free hand into a fist. If Drae launched an attack on the Brownstone building and hurt anyone, Alison might not care about disrupting Drow politics. She'd only stayed out of everything as much as possible because she thought it would make things worse.

Rasila frowned and stood. She narrowed her eyes and muttered something about cowardice.

"Yes, a Drow," Ava replied. "He's not made any direct threats, but he's rather insistent about your immediate presence. What should I tell him?"

What? Drae can't pick up a phone?

She looked over at her companion. "Tell him I'll be right there."

CHAPTER TWENTY-TWO

Alison ended the call and dropped her phone into her pocket. "I need you to portal us to outside the Brownstone Building. To be clear, I don't expect you to back me if things get violent. Even if it is Drae, this is an attack on me, not you."

Rasila scoffed. "I choose my fights, Princess of the Shadow Forged. You're not my queen yet, and you can't order me away. If Drae chooses to attack you and I choose to intervene, isn't that my choice?"

"Is that your roundabout way of saying you want to help?"

"Make of it what you will. Let's find out what's going on." The Drow raised her hands and began to chant, murmuring quick incantations.

She licked her lips and murmured her own spell. The flows of Rasila's magic grew visible and allowed Alison to better follow their manipulation and the other princess's shadow compression techniques. Both Rasila and Miar had practiced portal spells with her, but despite her high magical power, she had yet to stabilize one.

I'm so close. I merely need to continue practicing and observing. Everything that's happened lately shows that I have to learn how to portal.

A dark dot ringed with purple opened in front of them and expanded to frame the front door of the Brownstone Building on the other side. Two humanoid forms were visible through the front windows.

"Are you sure?" Rasila asked, her face set in grim determination. "What happens in the next few minutes might very well start us all down a path that we can't escape. This is a Drow matter, Alison. It will likely end in bloodshed."

She nodded and took a deep breath. "That little misadventure in Mongolia reminded me of something very important. Sometimes, no matter how much you want to avoid a fight, you can't. I'm Alison Brownstone and sometimes, I have to do things the way my dad did things."

"I'm glad you understand. May you have the lethal prowess of your father in the coming days."

The two women stepped briskly through the portal and the arcane opening snapped shut behind them. They nodded to each other and strode toward the front doors. Both layered shields over their bodies, but neither summoned a weapon.

A tall Drow man in dark armor stood inside and stared at Ava with open disdain. He turned when the two entered the lobby and the corners of his mouth quirked up in a faint grin.

Rasila snorted and gestured to the Drow. "This one is Marat. He is loyal to Novati."

Marat bowed his head to Rasila and Alison in turn. "Greetings, Princess of the Endless Shadow and Princess of the Shadow Forged." His gaze lingered on Rasila. "This message is for Princess Alison, but you may bear witness."

"How magnanimous of you," Rasila muttered.

He inclined his head toward Ava. "But I will not deliver it in the presence of the human."

"If you need me, Miss Brownstone, call for me. I'll be cleaning a rifle." Ava offered her a slight nod before she walked down the hallway and disappeared into a conference room.

Despite the armor, the Drow didn't have a shield spell up nor any obvious weapons or battle spells readied. Alison's heart maintained a healthy gallop, but she worried less about an immediate assault. She and Rasila were already prepared for battle.

"What's your message?" she asked.

"I come with word from the most honorable and powerful Novati, Princess of the Dark Sun," Marat announced, his tone approaching that of a radio announcer. She almost laughed.

He's trying so hard, but I think he actually thinks he can intimidate me.

"I kind of assumed that," she replied. "But what's her actual message?"

First Drae and now Novati. Shit. Rasila's right. Stalling time's over. Bloodbath time is beginning.

"Princess Novati takes a dim view of cowardly manipulation and political maneuvering," Marat continued. The sneering disdain on his face directed toward Rasila was hard to miss. "She is aware that you, the Princess of the

Shadow Forged, refuse to commit either to the present regime or to yourself or other candidates for queen. She will not bend her knee to any princess who lacks the strength to face their opponents in direct battle. Therefore, she issues a formal challenge for you to bring three of your greatest warriors. She will face you and your warriors with her own in a fight to the death. In this way, she will determine who is worthy to be queen."

"She wants a death match?" Alison shook her head. "This is ridiculous."

"Death doesn't have to happen. My princess is merciful. She might accept surrender, but she can't guarantee someone won't be killed." He raised his chin and more smugness bled into his face. "If the loser survives, she will submit to a binding ritual and formally renounce her claim to the throne and support of any other than the winner. You may also agree to submit to the ritual and support her without fighting if you're afraid of either you or your allies being killed."

She squared her shoulders. Novati had sent her man to threaten her in her own building. She couldn't stand there and take the slap without reacting.

"And what if I refuse both offers?" she asked. "Your princess has made a number of assumptions."

Marat smiled and licked his lips. "If you refuse her generous offer, Princess Novati will attack this building and those around it with overwhelming force. You can choose to defend it or you can choose to let others die because you're a sniveling half-human coward. If you stay and fight, she will cease her attack once you're dead as long as your servants surrender."

Rasila laughed. "She's even more foolish than I thought."

Alison stared at the emissary, her lips slightly parted. A few seconds later, she managed a slight shake of her head. "Is she insane? If she launches a large-scale attack on a neighborhood in an American city, she risks not only King Oriceran's intervention but the American government getting involved. There are damned treaties in place." She slapped her hand on her chest. "Not to mention me and all my friends and family. Screw the government. Is she ready for war against the Brownstone family?"

The man shrugged and replied with a disappointed grunt. "Princess Novati doesn't seek unnecessary carnage, and she leaves the choice to you, Princess of the Shadow Forged. If you are so intent on refusing to give up your claim, then you should defend it as is proper. Hiding behind human governments, King Oriceran, or others makes you nothing but a coward, and no Drow will follow a coward."

"Don't you care about your mistress starting a war? A war that will cost Drow lives? That's what we're talking about here."

"Maybe the Drow need a war!" Marat thundered, his eyes wide in the way only a true believer could manage. "My princess understands that if you and the other ineffectual princesses will not support her, she will need to unite our people in another way. We've been weak, lazy, stupid, and decadent since the Guardians took over. What do we have as options? A human playing at being a Drow, a fool who supports the Guardians, a coward who skulks in the shadows, and a weak princess who couldn't even defeat a half-human." He scoffed at Rasila.

She gave him a thin smile. "What's to stop me from killing Novati during this little battle? I value Alison's life far more than Novati's."

"You will be given your chance to face her," he promised balefully. "But if you attempt to intervene in this honorable duel, the princess will be compelled to commit all her forces, and the war will begin. You pride yourself on seeing so much in your webs of information, Princess Rasila, so you should know how many are willing to follow Princess Novati. The Drow crave strength, and she provides it. Unlike you or this half-human whelp."

Alison snickered. "Whelp? That's the first time anyone called me that. Maybe you can shake your fist at me and tell me to get off your lawn."

Marat spun on his heel and stormed toward the front doors. "I will return in one day. Have your answer ready, Princess of the Shadow Forged, or have your forces prepared to die." He threw the door open and strode outside, glaring at some poor woman in yoga pants jogging with her cocker spaniel.

"You should have struck him down where he stood." Rasila watched him walk up the street.

"That would have ended in the same thing—an attack on this building." Alison rubbed her temples. "Damn it. I have no choice, do I? That bitch has boxed me in."

"If you take her challenge, you minimize the risk to others." Her companion shrugged. "I'm less concerned with non-Drow deaths than you, but we both know, given your predilections, that you don't have another choice. If you contact the government or if you attempt to bring your father, war will begin anyway. Innocent people will suffer. He's right. That would be a form of cowardice."

"If I take Novati's challenge, I'll basically declare that I should be queen," she added resentfully. "I'll end up trapped even further by Drow politics."

"True, but you could die in the process," Rasila pointed out.

"Aren't you the cheerful one?" Alison resisted the urge to stamp her feet. "If I do this, I need my friends to volunteer, which means I can't know one way or another until I've talked to them. I might be their boss, but I won't order them into a death match with the Drow."

Rasila sighed. "You're far too concerned with democracy and feelings. Very well. I would suggest taking some time and sleeping on it. You have a day in which to decide. Novati will almost certainly want to fight somewhere on Oriceran. I will insist that I be the one to open the portal for you."

She frowned. "Why?"

"Novati is obsessed with her martial prowess, but she's not Miar. I don't put it above her to try some kind of trick, even if she lacks Drae's subtlety."

"Do you think she'll agree to that?"

The other woman's greedy grin disturbed her.

"Yes, because she's vain, too. I'll offer my witnessing as a temptation and refuse otherwise. She'll want all the other princesses to see this battle. She's probably already in the process of inviting the others." Rasila stared at her, something cold and calculating in her eyes. "She hasn't earned an assassination yet with her behavior, but I'm willing to entertain the pos—"

"No." Alison shook her head firmly. "If we want to stop a civil war, we need to do this in a way that other Drow will respect. I'm not sure if I'll end up fighting her here or there, but she'll see me coming if I have to kill her. That's the way I do things. I'm a security contractor who sometimes does bounty hunting and a little tomb raiding, but I'm not an assassin."

Rasila nodded slowly, slight disappointment in her eyes. "I understand. I will return tomorrow."

She stared at her for a few more seconds before she opened a portal and stepped through it, her face set in grim resignation.

"Damn it," Alison muttered. "I wanted to get through one week without starting a war."

CHAPTER TWENTY-THREE

There was no other option but to take Rasila's advice and sleep on the problem, although she did explain the situation to Mason. To her surprise, he said he would wait to offer his opinion until the morning meeting. It was nice to have a man who would give her time to think, especially considering the gravity of the situation.

It only took her a few brief minutes to explain everything the next morning. She'd commandeered the conference room and brought in Hana, Mason, and Drysi, the three people she would have chosen, along with Tahir for his perspective. She'd half-considered contacting Lily and Izzie, but although she trusted them, they didn't deserve to be dragged into her Drow garbage, especially Izzie who finally tasted freedom after so many years of being on the run.

Beyond that, her friends at Brownstone Security weren't merely friends. They were men and women she'd fought beside on many dangerous jobs. Their small team had trained together so much that explicit orders and strategies were often not even necessary in most situations. Everyone knew each other's capabilities, and they all knew what they needed to do in a fight. Hana, Mason, and Drysi were, in every sense, her champions.

The life wizard sighed and avoided looking at Alison. "There's one choice that avoids trouble, but you won't like it. Still, I think we should at least discuss it."

"What's that?" she asked and her stomach tightened.

He's worried about me, but this is about more than only me now.

"You could agree to her demands." He looked up and met her gaze.

Hana rolled her eyes. "Alison won't become Novati's lackey. That's super-stupid. No offense."

Alison frowned. "I wouldn't have put it that way, but Hana's right. This isn't simply a matter of me agreeing to stay neutral like I attempted to do before. My choice is to fight or actively support her. Either way, the balance that's kept all this Drow crap from blowing up is gone. Whatever I choose may end up indirectly deciding who becomes the next Drow queen."

This had better not end with me becoming queen.

"And you're sure you don't want to support Novati?" Drysi asked and folded her arms. "If she has enough followers that she's confident about starting a war, it might not hurt to get on her good side. It might be that the decision's already been made."

She shook her head. "I've not heard anything good about her. Not only from Miar and Rasila but also when I was on Oriceran. Besides, she's a Laena supporter. This all might end up a prelude to Laena becoming queen again, and if she does, it essentially guarantees open season on all things Brownstone, including friends and family. Even if she didn't support Laena, I'll never back a woman who would threaten a massacre to force someone to fight them. She's ruthless and brutal, and I won't tolerate someone like that."

The Welshwoman shrugged. "I'm not saying she's not a right bitch but wanted to toss that out there to chew on. You know I have no problem killing assholes, regardless of species."

Alison raised a tightly clenched fist. "And to be honest, I'm pissed at this point. I tried my hardest to stay neutral. I tried to let the Drow sort it out, but everyone has targeted me anyway. Miar and Rasila weren't so bad, but if what Rasila's people reported is true, I have Drae trying to arrange backdoor assassinations and Novati preparing to massacre people to draw me out. If I somehow agree to this stupid binding ritual and still try to sit it out, Drae might send her assassins anyway, but if I defeat Novati, that'll least send a message that these people aren't free to mess with me and mine."

Hana smiled. "I have your back, no matter what. I bet Novati doesn't even like mini-golf and has terrible fashion sense. Screw her."

Mason nodded with an expression of firm resolve. "You're right. You've tried your best to stay out of it, A, but it's obvious now that this doesn't end with them agreeing to sit down and talk it out. At least this way, you can start going on the offensive. Also, at this point, there are still the three other princesses who can help contain things if they get out of hand, and two of them like you."

Tahir furrowed his brow in deep thought. He tapped his phone and muttered under his breath for a few seconds before he raised his voice. "And are you confident that you can beat this Novati? From what you've told us, she's supposed to be far more battle-inclined and therefore perhaps more skilled than some of the other princesses."

"If I can stand toe-to-toe with Miar and Rasila, I can take Novati." She nodded to Drysi, Hana, and Mason in turn. "And I know they can win against whatever Drow she brings with her. We've all fought Drow together and won before."

Tahir's gaze lingered on Hana, along with a slight frown. Alison understood how he felt. Unlike Mason, he wasn't a strong battle wizard, and they wouldn't be allowed to include any drones in the challenge. He would trust her to take his lover into battle and come back with her still alive.

I'm sorry, Tahir. I wish there were another way.

"I can ask you to do this," she finally said softly, "but I can't order you to. We're not talking about a job, and there's no client. Novati and her goons will try to kill us, but the more I think about it, the more I believe that this is the only way I can solve this problem. Even if I let them kill me, Novati or Drae can't become queen."

Mason glared at her. "You don't get to pull a martyr complex on me, A. Don't even think about giving yourself up. I didn't marry you so you can throw your life away out of some misguided attempt to protect people who can do that quite capably themselves."

Hana nodded firmly. "What he said. I'm tired of all these crazy princesses. You've put your life on the line for me and even Omni a number of times. I owe you more than I can ever pay back, Alison. If it weren't for you, I'd be —" She sucked in a breath. "Let's kick some Drow ass, okay?"

Drysi shrugged. "If it weren't for you, I'd still be running around doing the Seventh Order's bidding. That would be annoying because of all the bastards I had to deal with. I have so much to make up for and I need your help to do that, which means I need you to stay alive."

Tahir set his phone down. "Given what we've experienced concerning Drae and Novati, you may very well be the only person who can stop them from doing something idiotic that results in a war. Risking a small number of people makes more sense. I only regret that I can't help more directly. Being an infomancer is a disadvantage in this situation."

Alison locked eyes with each of her friends in turn and her heart swelled with pride. "It sounds like we're all in agreement."

They nodded.

"I'll call Rasila. Now, we wait for Marat."

CHAPTER TWENTY-FOUR

About six hours later, Alison stepped through Rasila's large portal onto a boulder-strewn field. Tall snow-capped mountain peaks loomed in the distance. The rocky wasteland extended for miles in every direction dotted with a few shrubs and sad, broken trees as the only vegetation.

At least Novati chose a place where no innocent people would be hurt. I'll give her a little credit for that, but only a little. She shouldn't have come looking for a fight if she didn't want to get hurt.

Three small groups of Drow waited twenty yards away, all wearing dark armor. Most were unarmed but some carried swords. One man held a large curved silver blade, the shaft of which was as long as his body. Given the fact that the groups stood several yards apart and the different heraldry on their armor, they weren't together.

Miar stood at the center of one group, her sword at her side. She offered Alison a polite nod. An amused-looking Drae stood with another group and cast a glance at the new arrivals before she whispered to her entourage. Several of them laughed and gestured at the team.

Yeah, keep laughing. I'm here for Novati today, but don't think I won't look into this mysterious Drow pretending to be a Wood Elf.

Novati watched Alison with a broad smirk, her arms folded over her dark breastplate. The broad-shouldered, muscular woman was at least a good head taller than most of the Drow around her. Surprisingly, she didn't carry a magical sword like Miar.

Hana, Mason, and Drysi followed Alison through the portal, their defensive artifacts and primary weapons all ready. Everyone wanted to be sure they wouldn't be ambushed the minute they stepped onto Oriceran. The wizard and witch had both brought along nothing but anti-magic magazines along with casting all their enhancement spells. The *tachi* rested comfortably in Hana's sheath, but she hadn't foxed out yet.

"Woah." Hana gasped and pointed at the sky. "It's so different seeing it in person."

Two moons hung above them and even though the blue color of the sky and the local flora weren't exotic, there was no mistaking it. They were on Oriceran.

Alison took a deep breath. It was subtle, but it was almost like she could feel the higher level of background magic in the air. The Drow wouldn't have a major advantage, given that Drysi, Mason, and Alison would all have access to the same magical power, but Hana might be at a slight disadvantage.

"It's fucking weird," the Welshwoman muttered. "What's the point of two moons? More complicated tides?"

"We have planets in our solar system with more moons than that." She shrugged and wondered how they'd been sidetracked into an astronomy discussion.

"But we don't fight on them." Drysi muttered something else in Welsh.

Mason tilted his head. "I'll have to do a painting of that. Hana's right. It is striking to see in person."

"Welcome to Oriceran," Rasila offered and gestured grandly toward the moons.

Alison hadn't thought much about it, but none of her friends had ever been to Earth's magical sister planet. Technically, there was supposed to be significant paperwork involved in any interplanetary travel, but she had sent Ava to coordinate with Agent Latherby to make sure they at least had a bureaucratic fig leaf to cover the excursion. They didn't have time to wait for the rusty gears of the government to turn. She didn't want the agent to know how close the Drow were to committing terrorist acts against the United States, but she asked Ava to make it clear that it was important that the matter be handled in a prompt manner.

"I congratulate you, Princess of the Shadow Forged," Novati bellowed. "I'd wondered if you would run or hide behind your precious human servants. You might be considered a great woman on Earth, but this is Oriceran."

Yeah, yeah, keep telling yourself that.

She shrugged. "I'm here, along with my champions. You forced my hand, but someone needs to stop you before you do something stupid that results in the deaths of too many people. That might as well be me, and since you pissed me off, I'll probably enjoy it."

Drysi grinned.

Novati's mouth curled into a sneer. "The strong should rule. That's the way of the Drow. You would know that if you were a real Drow and not merely a freak." She gestured around her. "And now all the princesses have gathered. There can be no question what this challenge represents." She pointed to a slender robed woman standing near Miar's entourage. "Even the Guardians have sent an observer. The future of our people will be determined by this challenge, Alison Brownstone."

The slender Drow woman stepped forward. "I am Cerin. The Guardians have empowered me to make it clear that they do not commit to any course of action based on the events occurring here and have yet to issue a formal position on the nature and role of the Drow princesses. They maintain that continued dialog is necessary to determine the future of our people and encourage the princesses to support the stability the Guardians have provided following the fall of Laena."

"Guardians? What a bizarre name for a group of sniveling cowards." Novati snickered. "They want others to kill for them but they won't risk themselves. It's fine. You can report to them how I destroyed a threat to both their power and mine and they will understand that they will have no choice but to serve me."

"Why do you even care?" Alison scoffed. "The way I hear it, you're a Laena supporter. What's the point of proving your power if you'll simply turn it over to her? And you plan to do that despite the fact that my Dad kicked her ass on her home turf."

Scattered Drow glared at her. A few muttered under their breaths.

That's right. Remember who I am. I'm not merely a random woman or even a random princess. I'm Alison fucking Brownstone, and you assholes made me come here.

"Your monstrous adopted father was lucky, Princess of the Shadow Forged. It won't happen again. He's not even a warrior anymore."

"If you think that's what his retirement means, you're beyond deluded."

Novati lowered her arms and stared at her while some unidentifiable emotion played across her face. "It doesn't matter. My current battle is with you. I believe the Drow were stronger with Queen Laena leading us. I intend to unite all the Drow through force, and then I intend to let her challenge me. If she is stronger, she will take my place. The natural order of things will be restored, not this mockery that we've allowed to continue since the unfortunate interference of James Brownstone."

Miar and the Guardian representative frowned deeply. Rasila shook her head and muttered while Drae smiled broadly as if the entire display was the most amusing thing she'd witnessed in weeks.

Do you think there'll be one less competitor for you, Drae? Don't worry. You're next on the list.

Novati pointed at Alison. "I'll give you one last chance, Princess of the Shadow Forged. Pledge your loyalty to me and I'll spare your life and those of your pathetic servants. As my ally, I'll never threaten your friends or family. I'll also spare the life of your father as long as I'm queen, but I can't speak for Laena should she best me."

She laughed. "Are you serious right now? Or is this a sophisticated Drow joke that I don't understand?"

The aggressive princess gritted her teeth. "Are you so confident of victory?"

"I think if you attack my father, you'll face my father and my mother." Alison shook her head. "I'm not sure even I can defeat both of them, but you're right. It doesn't matter because this is the part where we turn things around. You have to get through me before you get to my family, and that won't happen." She pointed at her own chest. "And I give you one last chance to back the hell off. I don't even want any fancy binding ritual or anything like that. I'm willing to make this simple. You don't mess with me and I don't mess with you. That's all I ask."

Her adversary snorted. "You're so weak and the wish was wasted on you. It sickens me. No. I refuse. If you run, I will pursue you and you will die either way. Let us end this as warriors and not cowards." She pivoted on her heel and marched away from the crowd. Three Drow men stepped away from their group and fell in behind her. Two had no visible weapons, and the third carried the curved polearm blade. The weapon began to glow a dull orange.

Alison cracked her knuckles before she layered a few more shields over her body and conjured a shadow blade. "How many times do I need to defeat a Drow royal before you people get the damned point?"

CHAPTER TWENTY-FIVE

Alison, Hana, Drysi, and Mason positioned themselves across from Novati and her warriors, facing them from ten yards away. No one had mentioned any special rules and despite the obsession with martial valor, the Drow didn't have many formalized rituals concerning challenges. The most important rule for battle was also the simplest—destroy the enemy.

"I will enjoy killing you, Princess of the Shadow Forged," Novati stated with a hungry grin. "The cloud of the Brownstone name has hung over our people for far too long. Wiping it away will be the first step toward restoring us to what we should be." She raised her hands. Shadow wings appeared, and tendrils of shadow wound around each other to form shadow blades. Hers were shorter but thicker than what Alison preferred.

"No one touch Novati," she ordered. "I'll handle her myself."

"Excellent." Her adversary pointed her blades at her. "That's exactly what I want. Whether I take the throne or

Laena does, everything will change. The Drow are growing weak under the Guardians and outside pollution. You're a living example of that corruption. By destroying you, I'll destroy a symbol of both our humiliation and demonstrate the power of a true Drow over a champion of Earth."

"Keep talking. It simply fires me up, you arrogant bitch."

Novati's warriors spread out and each stood opposite a single member of the Brownstone team. Dark shields encased their bodies, but none of them conjured shadow wings. In the end, there was a noticeable difference between royals, elders, and the common Drow. As powerful as they were, they had their limits.

Is it purely about being that much better at shadow compression? At least it means my team won't be at a horrible disadvantage. This should go about as well as when we faced Rasila's people the first time, and they had better numbers.

Alison snorted. "I'll enjoy defeating you simply because you're so loud and obnoxious." She channeled shadow magic into her back and her dark shadow wings appeared. "You made a mistake when you threatened the people I care about, Novati. I've tried to stay out of this crap, but you all keep pulling me in. Congratulations, you've pissed me off way more than Rasila did when we first met, and that's saying something."

"Your mistake was being born, Alison Brownstone. And today, I end that mistake on behalf of my people." Novati elevated suddenly and dense purple-black lines coiled around her blades. Alison burst upward in the same moment that her opponent released two black beams that carved into the rocky soil.

Hana's tails appeared. Her claws grew and her eyes changed as she surged forward and drew her sword at the same time. She stabbed at a Drow, but he darted to the side, pushed by a dark, nebulous tentacle that rose from his shadow. He thrust his palm forward and three dark orbs careened toward the fox. Her quick movement saved her from what would have been direct strikes. They struck the ground and exploded. The Drow avoided her next attack with another helpful magical push.

They must have done their homework. He knows she can carve through his shield with that sword and is keeping mobile. Did they deliberately select to fight the person they thought they could most easily beat? For that to make sense, it means Novati spent considerable time studying me, but she doesn't seem the type.

Alison didn't have time to focus on her friends. That momentary lapse in concentration cost her as Novati's beams ripped into her shields. Burning pain suffused her side and she spun and flung several light bolts at the other princess. The brief respite was enough for her to pour shadow magic into the wound. The darkness swallowed the entire area and gradually retreated to reveal healed flesh. She concentrated more magic into her shields. The magic flowed noticeably easier than on Earth.

It's been a long time since I fought a Drow princess seriously. This isn't training. This woman wants to kill me.

Drysi sprinted in a circle around her enemy, the Drow with the long, curved blade. She drew her gun and fired, but his weapon spun in a blur and the bullet bounced off with a bright spark. Its wielder offered her a vicious grin.

"No fucking way," the witch shouted. "Those are anti-magic bullets." She tried a few more shots but each time, her bullet didn't reach its mark.

The Drow sneered. "You're overly reliant on your toy, Earth witch." He launched into the air, his weapon still spinning in front of him and held by his left hand. With a sharp gesture, he cut in front of him with his right hand. A thin crescent of purple-black energy, almost identical to one of the spells Alison used, winked into existence and hurtled toward Drysi. She grunted in pain when it caught her shoulder. Her shield saved her from serious injury, but the thin cut in her jacket was a testimony to the power of her opponent.

Mason had neither his gun nor his wand out. His enhanced speed had him well-matched with his quickly dodging opponent. The enemy's small rapid-fire orbs didn't explode like some of his allies' attacks, and the life wizard's erratic movements prevented them from landing. He closed on his adversary and drove a fist into him. His target catapulted several yards before he landed and bounded to his feet with a hiss.

"You'll die for that, wizard," the Drow screamed. "I'll gut you."

"Do before you talk," he retorted.

The two princesses continued their mutual strafing runs. They spun, dived, and rose rapidly as each tried to get a decent angle. A few of Alison's light bolts exploded against Novati, but other than a grimace, the Drow didn't react. Her counterattack clipped Alison's shoulder. The impact stung but her earlier reinforcement kept it from burning her.

Judging by Rasila and Miar, I won't win with my easy spells, especially on Oriceran.

She had shoved considerable magic into her shields. Maintaining her defenses, flying speed, and offense was taxing even with being on Oriceran, but Novati's expression had shifted from joy to one of grim determination. They now both pushed each other to their limits.

I need time to charge up, but she won't give it to me.

A grin swallowed the other princess's grim expression. She lowered her arms although she continued her hasty changes of direction to avoid Alison's stream of attacks. "You're wasting your energy, Alison. I'll simply wait until it's time. You might as well stop attacking."

"What the hell is that supposed to mean?" she shouted. "Are you giving up?"

Novati jerked back and one of Alison's shadow crescents missed her by less than an inch.

"A queen is only as good as her servants," the challenger replied. "I will wait until my men slay your pathetic Earth garbage, and then I'll destroy you as you whimper for mercy, your spirit broken after the death of your champions."

She brought her arm back for another attack but stopped. "That's your brilliant plan?"

"And you're weak and sentimental," Novati called in response. "That's why you shouldn't be queen. I know once your friends die, it'll be more enjoyable to destroy you. And that weak wizard is your husband, isn't he? Your disgusting human husband. If you had at least committed to your people, I might tolerate you, but you've chosen your loyalties."

"You're a real bitch. Did anyone ever tell you that?"

Hana raced constantly toward her opponent, but his magic-fueled movement turned him into a blurry shadow. He laughed with each missed swing.

"You should be happy, fox," he taunted. "You'll be dead soon and won't have to watch our princess destroy Alison Brownstone."

She growled and made two quick stabs. Both met nothing but air.

"I'd love to kill you cut by cut," she responded curtly, "but I think I'll simply kill you as quickly as possible because you're so fucking obnoxious." She swung her blade, and his shadow tentacle pushed him down again, his legs spread like he was a Drow Jean-Claude Van Damme.

Alison surveyed the battlefield. All her friends could use help. They'd let Novati bait them into a fight following her rhythms.

"I know what you're thinking, Alison," the other princess shouted. "You think this could end quickly if you helped, but if you make any move toward them, I'll attack you. You can't help your friends and keep your guard up. And I can tell you I'm not distracted with worry over my men, which means I'll win if you try to help."

Despite the burns and tears in Mason's shirt and the blood that streamed down the side of his head, he had an easier time with his opponent than Hana. His enemy swayed after receiving another mighty blow, his face battered. Every time he hesitated even for a moment to heal, the life wizard surged forward with punches and kicks. A faint glow surrounded his hands.

Oh, he decided to up his game, huh? Using extra magic isn't as big a deal one-on-one.

Drysi emptied her magazine into her enemy, but he deflected every shot.

Her opponent stalked toward her with his spinning blade. "Did you think I'd be so easy to defeat, witch? That a few enchanted bullets would be enough? Pathetic. I expected more of one of Alison Brownstone's warriors, but your reputation is nothing but smoke."

The Welshwoman tossed her gun in an arc and the Drow's gaze instinctively followed the weapon. She yanked two daggers from her jacket sheaths, one with a white glow and another with a red. The white one left her hand instantly on a direct trajectory toward the spinning blade, while she threw the red toward his shoulder on the opposite side.

The Drow's gaze raised and he focused on the white dagger. Arcs of light streaked from it on contact. The other dagger exploded and tumbled him. He landed hard with a groan and his blade spun from his hand when he impacted.

His weapon must actually have enhanced his reaction to what he saw coming rather than actually shielding him.

Drysi didn't retrieve her gun but instead, drew three red daggers in rapid succession and threw them at her opponent. The explosions swallowed him. She pulled a magazine out of her pocket and flung herself into a roll, snatched her weapon up, and slapped the new magazine in. It was already aimed at the explosion when she found her feet. The smoke and flame cleared and revealed the prone Drow. With a bloodthirsty scream, she charged and fired.

His body jerked with each hit, but she maintained her

advance until she was only a yard away and emptied the remainder of the magazine into his head.

"Come back from that, fucker," she muttered belligerently.

Hana continued her frustrated samurai imitation against her enemy. Several more thrusts missed until she feinted a slice before she spun to stab in the opposite direction. The Drow pushed himself directly into the path of her blade and it pierced his chest.

She didn't offer a witty quip or wait for his shadow healing to begin. With a vicious motion, she wrenched the *tachi* out and twisted to swing the blade at his neck. It carved through his flesh and bone and his head arced away from his body.

Mason battered his enemy relentlessly. The constant attacks kept the Drow off-balance, but his healing, as sporadic as it was, prevented him from being defeated. A rapid series of jabs careened him into a painful fall. The life wizard dropped to one knee and whipped his gun out. He shoved it against the Drow's head and pulled the trigger twice.

The Brownstone wizard stood and staggered a little as he wiped the blood out of his eyes. The team had defeated their enemies, but not without a cost. Lacerations and burns covered their bodies.

Novati stared at the carnage below, her eyes wide. "Impossible."

Alison snickered. It was time for a little psychological warfare. "If that's the quality of your champions, I'm not at all impressed with your army." She floated backward. "But they've done their part, and now it's my turn." She bowed in the air. "Are you ready to give up and pledge your loyalty to me, Novati?"

Pure hatred shone in the other woman's dark eyes. "Fine. I'll cripple you, but I'll leave you alive long enough so you can see me kill them."

In the distance, Cerin strolled away from the Drow observers. A portal opened, and she stepped through.

"Apparently, the Guardian rep saw everything she needed to." Alison grinned. "She knows how this will end. Bring it on, Novati. Let's finish this."

CHAPTER TWENTY-SIX

With a sudden sharp elevation, Alison flung a constant stream of light bolts at her adversary. Now that her friends had begun to retreat toward the gathered spectators without any threats, she could focus on defeating the other princess. This wouldn't be like her first battle with Rasila. If she didn't stop the Drow, her friends and family would be targeted.

Sometimes, you can come to an agreement and sometimes, you have to choke someone.

Novati darted out of the line of fire and turned faster than expected. She barreled into a concerted onslaught and didn't dodge the stream of light bolts that exploded against her shields. She grimaced and closed in on her opponent, who spun to dodge her attacker's thrusts.

Alison channeled more power into a new shadow blade and stabbed powerfully. The other woman parried her blow with one of her smaller blades before she slashed at Alison's shield. They exchanged several more blows and each weakened the other's shields but didn't draw blood.

An odd wave of magical pressure passed through the area. It didn't feel like it came from Novati's direction, but Alison shoved the thought aside. It was probably nothing more than witnesses using magic to get a better view of the action. A momentary lapse in concentration could end with her death.

She launched herself below her opponent and raised her free hand to channel both light and shadow magic into an orb. The other princess dived toward her, her blades ready and her face eager, but Alison released the attack.

The exploding orb careened the other Drow away before she righted herself and released the magic that fueled her blades. Several holes marred her armor and painful-looking burns lay beneath, but darkness spread over them immediately.

She's better at shadow healing than I am. I won't win a war of attrition.

Novati brought her arms back. Purple-tinged shadows threaded together into an impenetrably dark spear. She bellowed in rage and flung the weapon toward her enemy.

Alison jerked to the side, surprised at the straightforward attack. The spear changed direction and a yard away, it separated into seven smaller spears that pelted her. Two made it through her shields and bit into her legs and chest. She hissed in pain but didn't focus magic on healing. Instead, she gritted her teeth, shut her eyes, and murmured an incantation.

A small spark exploded into a bright flash in front of her opponent. Alison snapped her eyes open and followed up with a surge toward her foe. She streaked forward with a burst of magic, her blade pointed directly ahead. Her onslaught powered through Novati's weakened shields, and the tip of her blade emerged out the other side of the Drow's abdomen.

The princess growled in pain and thrust back as she raised her hands. Blood seeped from her wound. Alison's continued attack was disrupted when her adversary slapped her hands together and shouted an incantation. A blue-black explosion pounded into the princesses and flung them in opposite directions, both smoking and their shields depleted.

Damn, that hurt, but it's time to take a chance.

She rocketed up and ceased feeding her wings. For the moment, she didn't bother to restore her shields or use even a small amount of magic for healing. Burns and cuts covered her body and every part of her hurt, but that was the trade-off.

When she reached the end of her upward thrust, she let herself fall and shoved magical energy into a twisting lance streaked with dark lines. The half-blinded Novati didn't immediately retaliate. Instead, she righted herself in the air and reinforced her shields. It took only a few seconds, but it was enough for Alison to launch her next assault.

The magical weapon screamed toward Novati. It cut through her shields and tore a huge hole in her chest that showered a spray of blood. Her wings disappeared, and she tumbled toward the ground.

Raw power was important for a fight, but when two people were matched, the superior tactician would come out on top.

Alison plummeted and reached the rocky ground before her foe. She extended her wings to break her fall but

Novati didn't and landed with a loud thud. Although she didn't move, tendrils of shadow stretched to fill her gaping wound.

I have to give it to her. That's impressive. It's almost Dad-level regeneration.

She thrust the thought aside, dragged in a deep breath, and raised her arms. This time, she forced every scrap of magic she could gather into a growing blue-white orb of pure explosive destruction. If she couldn't win by blowing through most of her opponent's chest, she would make sure there was nothing left to regenerate. The stabbing and burning pain from her wounds distracted her and the sensation grew more intense as she called on greater power.

Her baseball-sized orb of doom became a basketball and then a beach ball. Dark shadows covered most of Novati's body and confirmed that she wasn't out of the fight.

"I gave you your chance." Alison hissed and released the attack. The massive orb rocketed toward the other princess and bright arcs of white and blue light crackled over its surface.

Novati's head turned and her lips moved, but without her lungs, no words emerged. The projectile struck her and exploded to drive out a massive shockwave and a shower of dirt and rock. The force of the blast pounded into Alison and flung her off her feet. She landed with a crunch and slid several yards, her vision blurry and her ears ringing.

Someone dark and fuzzy came into her line of sight. She wasn't sure how much time had passed. Warmth spread over her body, and her pain began to subside.

Mason's concerned voice broke through the residual tinnitus. "A, you all right?"

Alison blinked a few times to clear her vision. Her husband crouched beside her, his wand pressed against her body. Her clothes were a shredded, burned mess, but most of her wounds had already healed.

She groaned and sat up. Her attack had produced a huge smoking crater.

"And Novati?" she asked. "I'd hate to think I did all that work for nothing."

"There's nothing left of her." He shrugged. "I don't know if her body turned into black mist or not like Myna's did. It was hard to tell with all the smoke." He extended a hand to help her up.

With his support, she stood and turned toward the other Drow. Some of Novati's people knelt on one knee, their heads bowed. Others looked stunned.

Good. At least we don't have to fight them.

Slowly, she walked toward the gathered Drow. "Is everyone satisfied? Two princesses entered, one princess left."

Miar hurried to her and clapped her on the shoulder. "Magnificent, Alison. You are a true warrior."

Rasila chuckled. "Novati was always too straightforward, a fatal flaw in battle."

Drae offered her a cold smile. She looked far too satisfied with herself. "This finally ends your feeble claims of neutrality, Princess of the Shadow For—"

A towering pyramid made of what appeared to be yard-thick frosted glass materialized around the gathered people and trapped everyone inside. The ground rumbled, and the top layer of rock and dirt transmuted into the same material.

Alison stumbled forward and her stomach churned as the world spun for a moment. Waves of tremendous magical power pulsed through the area. They were even stronger than what she'd felt in Mongolia.

"Yeah, this isn't good." She turned slowly from one side to the other in search of someone outside the pyramid to blame. There was no one there.

The assembled Drow didn't waste time discussing things. They went to the immediate Drow response—destruction. Several attacked the pyramid with shadow blades and hacked wildly. Others flung fireballs, cutting shadow crescents, or even bubbling acid in their attempts to break free. A few chanted more complicated destruction spells.

Hana drew her *tachi* and swung at a wall. Her blade bounced off and left only a thin scratch. Mason and Drysi both drew their wands and launched fireballs, but their attacks inflicted little more than a light charring.

Rasila frowned and raised her hands. She began to murmur the incantation for a portal, but nothing appeared.

A minute passed during which the elite Drow and Brownstone team attempted to break through before Drae threw her head back and laughed. Everyone stopped their efforts and stared at her with a mixture of horror and curiosity.

The laughter died, but the bright, amused smile on her face didn't leave. "I can't be the only one who realizes what's happened, can I?"

"Why don't you share with the rest of the class then,

genius?" Alison asked. She hissed as another magical wave passed over her. Several Drow shuddered, and Hana gagged.

It's not only me.

"Who is no longer with us?" Drae asked.

"Novati?" Alison answered. "Are you saying this is some kind of final revenge spell?"

Drae snorted. "You vaporized her. I can see why you don't understand. Perhaps you didn't notice during your battle." She glared at Miar. "But one of us left before it was completed, the one representative of a group that had a unique opportunity with all five princesses gathered in one place and distracted."

Her breath caught. "Are you saying this is the work of the Guardians?"

The other woman nodded and her smile finally turned to a look of disgust. "I was a fool. I suggested to them they might want to send a representative to this gathering, but I never thought they would be ruthless enough to try something like this. Of course, they would wait until one of you had killed the other. It'd be the point of maximum distraction. I'd thought there was unusual magical flow during the battle, but with two Drow princesses fighting, it was hard to tell."

Miar shook her head, disbelief carved into her features. "They wouldn't do this."

Drae scoffed. "Why? Because they're so honorable, Miar? You were a fool to ever trust them." She gestured toward the nearest wall. "You all sense it. This isn't merely a temporary containment spell. Go ahead and try to open a portal if you can."

Mason moved closer to Alison. He kept his wand out and watched the Drow with suspicion.

Miar and Rasila both raised their hands and all but shouted their portal incantations. Nothing happened.

The two princesses exchanged looks of grim resignation.

Drysi walked over to the wall and kicked it. She frowned. "Right. That won't work. Somehow, I'm not surprised that I'll die blown up in a fucking Oriceran magical glass pyramid. Here lies Drysi Jones. She should simply have stayed a right bastard assassin."

Hana sheathed her blade. She clawed at the glass before she growled her frustration. "This can't be happening. There's a whole group of Drow princesses here. Can't you all use your royal magic or something?"

Miar looked at the ground with a pained expression. "I felt resistance when I tried to open the portal. If there's resistance, we have a chance to overwhelm it with magical power." She raised her hands. "But Hana's right. We have a narrow window in which to combine our magic."

Drae nodded. "I don't intend to die after being tricked by the Guardians. It's too humiliating." She raised her arms and nodded to her Drow. "Provide what you can. Rasila, Miar, have your people also perform a channeling ritual. I'll attempt to open a short-range portal. Miar's right. We might be able to force our way through."

"I'll open the portal anchor, and you can feed into it," Miar suggested, weariness in her tone. "We need to hurry."

The background magical pressure continued to build. Sparks rained from the top of the pyramid. Rays of light danced and twisted around each other high above like a living sculpture. Whatever it was, it grew steadily larger with each passing second.

Rasila stepped forward, an easy fluidity in her step. "At least we all now know who our mutual enemies are."

The other Drow spread out around Miar, Rasila, and Drae in a circle and began careful motions with their hands while they chanted. Alison might not be able to open a portal under normal circumstances, but she'd learned Drow channeling rituals during her time on Oriceran, and they were reinforced by Myna. It was a skill she had few opportunities to use, given that Miar and Rasila didn't go on jobs with her.

She joined the circle. "I'll direct the flow."

Hana and Drysi joined Mason near Alison but remained silent. Distraction wouldn't help anyone survive, and for all their power and skill, they weren't familiar with the ritual.

Lines of purple energy erupted from the Drow and connected each magical being. Additional lines sprang from them and converged on Alison. A burning sensation consumed her entire body, but she concentrated on focusing the energy. A thick, twisting column of energy launched from her hands before it flowed into three new lines to the other three princesses.

Drae and Rasila stood behind Miar and all chanted in unison.

Miar held her arms outstretched and kept her eyes closed. Sweat dripped down her face as she continued to cast her portal spell.

Alison wouldn't let a single thought sneak into her

head. She concentrated on acting as a conduit for all the magical power that rushed through her.

A dark uneven, jagged shape appeared in front of Miar. It twitched in the air and grew larger. A few seconds passed before it grew again. A murky darkness covered it, but even through that, the rocky fields outside the pyramid were visible.

The top of the structure illuminated. The sparks grew larger and fell almost in a waterfall now. The twisted nexus of light filled half the pyramid. Alison fought the urge to throw up as her stomach churned. She was unsure if it was from the background magical pressure or her role in the ritual.

Miar screamed in defiance. The portal wrenched open a little further. It was now large enough for people to make it through.

"Run!" she shouted. "I can only hold it for so long."

The Drow broke from the ritual circle and rushed through the aperture. Alison took a few deep breaths. Less power flowed through her but she was still dizzy from the growing magical pressure.

She nodded at Hana, Mason, and Drysi and flung her arm toward the portal. "Go!"

The two women sprinted through the new escape route. Her husband rushed toward her and grabbed her arm. He tugged, and they both sprinted with Drae and Rasila on their heels.

Alison and Mason ran through and collided with a panting Drow. The other two princesses stumbled out a second later.

The pyramid towered over them close by, Miar's

outline still visible and the light bright and intense. The nexus flared and consumed the entire inside of the pyramid and the portal vanished.

"Where the hell is Miar?" Alison shouted and her pulse pounded in her ears.

Several of Miar's warriors rushed forward, wide-eyed.

The pyramid glowed for several seconds before the light vanished. Small cracks slithered and spread throughout the exterior before the entire structure collapsed in a pile of sharp fragments.

Alison fell to her knees. There was no escaping the truth. Miar was gone.

CHAPTER TWENTY-SEVEN

Furious, Alison strode over to Drae. "Give me one good reason why I shouldn't kill you where you stand," she demanded.

The other woman's warriors all rushed behind their princess. The Drow serving Miar and Novati ran to either side of Alison. They all glared at Drae and her people.

"A, be careful," Mason warned.

Sorry. It's time to handle this like Daddy's little girl.

Despite his words, he had his wand out, as did Drysi. Hana kept her hand on the hilt of her sword and flexed her fingers.

The Drow serving Rasila turned toward their princess. She nodded slowly before she inclined her head toward Alison. Her warriors jogged over to reinforce those of the other two princesses who had perished.

With one small action, the duel before would turn into a bloodbath involving dozens of people.

Drae offered a condescending smile. "Don't you need to provide a good reason to kill me, Princess of the Shadow

Forged? Or are you so drunk on the blood of Novati that you're ready to remove your other competition immediately?" She gestured toward the small army behind Alison. "You could do it, you know. Your current allied forces would overwhelm mine. Everyone knows Rasila is ready to bend her knee to you, and Miar might not have supported you as queen but she was your friend."

"And now she's dead," Alison shouted, so angry that a little spittle escaped with the words. "Because of you. If you hadn't told the Guardians, they wouldn't have set the trap up, and maybe that wasn't even an accident. Like the mysterious Drow who took the form of a Wood elf and directed the Shadows of Rurik to me."

Drae sighed. "I never knew you were so paranoid."

"You get that way after about the fiftieth time someone tries to kill you."

Drae raised an eyebrow. "If you have proof that I arranged either of these incidents, present it. Otherwise, consider what you are saying. If you believe I was involved in this, it doesn't make sense. I told the Guardians so they could come and kill me, too?" She shook her head and her face twitched into a deep scowl. "I've admitted something important that I rarely do, Princess of the Shadow Forged. I made a mistake by not anticipating that they would take such a bold action. Actually, I made two mistakes."

She clenched her hands into fists. "And what was the second?"

"I should have killed the Guardians a long time ago." Drae gestured for her people to stand down. "I won't deny that this has worked out to my general advantage, but I'm not one to risk my life in unnecessary gambits.

Think past your rage, Princess Alison. We've seen who the enemy is. You've proven yourself worthy in battle. Novati's warriors have already acknowledged you. There are three of us left, all worthy of being queen, but there is one group of cowards who are not worthy, one group whose representative fled the field of battle at the point of maximum distraction. The conclusion is obvious."

"The damned Guardians." She knew where they would be. They'd set themselves up in Laena's palace following her defeat. She'd spoken to some of them there when she trained on Oriceran.

Drow royalty aren't the only ones who need to understand they can't screw with me.

Alison took a few deep breaths and raised her hand. She guided them through the intricate motions she'd practiced with Myna, Miar, and Rasila on countless occasions. The gestures pulled threads of shadow magic together and tightened and wove them toward her purpose. Finesse had always failed her in the past and she had never been able to manage the level of compression and concentration needed. Her fiery rage was now like a laser as she uttered the incantation.

A portal erupted in front of her. On the other side lay a long, dark bridge that stretched over a massive cavern. Four guards stood on the structure. The spires of the Drow palace protruded beyond a plateau that lay on the far side of the bridge.

She wasn't surprised. After all, she was a Brownstone and that meant sometimes, she merely needed a little anger.

Hana pumped her fist in the air. "Damn. No one can stop you now."

"That's right. They can't." Alison strode through the portal. She didn't maintain the energy flows and it snapped closed behind her. The four guards scrutinized her warily. Considering the wretched state of her clothes, they had to be confused about why she was there.

Oh, shit. I forgot everyone else.

Two portals opened and the other Drow marched through, their rhythmic footfalls echoing throughout the cavern. Drysi, Hana, and Mason followed them. Drae and Rasila appeared last and their respective portals closed behind them.

"Get the hell out of my way," Alison ordered the sentinels. "You do not want to fuck with me right now."

Rasila advanced, her chin raised in haughty disdain. "You heard the Princess of the Shadow Forged. She could easily kill you herself, but are you ready to face three Drow princesses and some of their most skilled warriors?"

The guards swallowed and stepped aside.

"A good choice," Rasila declared.

Alison continued without a word. She conjured a shadow blade and layered new shields over herself. Even though she was emotionally and physically exhausted, she would be ready for battle. If the Guardians wanted war, they could have it.

Her vengeful army crossed the bridge and stepped onto a road resembling polished obsidian. It wasn't slick, despite the appearance. Glowing crystal towers stood on either side. The path itself extended directly to the palace in the distance. There was an eerie beauty to the place she had appreciated when she'd spent time there before but now, she didn't care about anything but finding the Guardians.

A crowd of Drow, including dozens of men and women in armor, rushed down the path. Several wore the intricate robes of the Guardians. Cerin walked with them.

When Alison threw a hand up, the Drow following her halted as one. She raised her shadow blade.

One of the Guardians, a tall, withered Drow woman named Edra, nodded to a group of soldiers.

"Don't do anything you'll regret in the next few minutes," Alison warned. "Unless you're really looking forward to dying."

The soldiers conjured shadow blades and put them to the necks and back of Cerin and four of the other Guardians, three men and a woman. They shoved them forward.

What the—

A murmur rippled through the Drow gathered in front of Alison. None of her people said anything. They all looked as confused as she felt.

"On your knees," Edra shouted to the prisoners.

The moment of hesitation passed quickly with the threat of the soldiers behind them.

Alison released her blade. When her father was angry, he had his evil Jiminy Cricket in the form of his symbiont urging him to rage and violence. Without that input, the confusion over the scene sapped her anger.

"I'll ask one question," she began forthrightly. "If you try to bullshit me, this won't end well for many people."

Edra nodded slowly, pulled her shoulders back, and raised her head in a regal stance. Alison didn't speak to her much during her time on Oriceran, but she'd always thought the woman wasn't a total piece of garbage. She might have been wrong.

"Do you deny that the Guardians attempted to assassinate all the princesses?"

The Drow shook her head. "I don't deny that, but I want to make it clear it was not sanctioned by all the Guardians. The rest of us didn't know they had hatched such a plan." She inclined her head toward Cerin and her masters. "We don't condone what happened. I swear to you we did not know. We'll submit to truth magic if you don't believe me."

Her gaze bored into the woman and she had to grant her respect. Three angry princesses had arrived with a small army. One alone was worth dozens of Drow. If Alison, Rasila, and Drae decided to rampage, many people would die.

Cerin glared at her. "You are the past. Laena haunts us because she continues to live. At least if you relics had died as well, we could move forward. We can't wait for you to kill each other."

"The Guardians offer these lives as a show of good faith," Edra announced.

Alison stared at her in surprise. She'd been so angry and inspired to get her revenge but now, things had turned more complicated than she'd expected.

Rasila strode toward the prisoners and conjured a long, wide shadow blade. "Did you really think we were so weak?" She decapitated Cerin with one clean stroke. No shadows covered the wound and healed it. Alison grimaced. Four quick strikes finished the others. The princess executioner stepped back and released her blade.

Wow. She didn't even hesitate. I like her, but I forget how ruthless she can be.

Edra's gaze lingered on the headless bodies on the obsidian path. "I apologize again for this incident, but it's over now."

Drae chuckled. "Why should it end?"

Alison frowned and turned to look at her. "The people responsible are dead. There's obviously a considerable amount we all need to talk about, but the ass-kicking portion of this meeting is now over."

The other Drow princess sighed with her usual dislike. "Short-term thinking will forever be your bane, Princess of the Shadow Forged. There are three of us here, along with our allies. We could kill the rest of the Guardians right now. Why wait?"

The Guardians' warriors stepped back and summoned shields or shadow blades. Those with magical swords, axes, and blades readied them. Some weapons burst into flame while dark nimbuses surrounded others. The princesses' army mirrored them.

Oh, shit. The civil war is about to start.

"They didn't do it," Alison insisted, her heart thundering. She looked from one army to the other. "Killing the people who tried to kill us is one thing, but killing those who haven't done anything is something else entirely. I refuse to participate in that."

Drae shook her head with undisguised glee on her face. "All you're doing is delaying the inevitable. You made the choice, Princess of the Shadow Forged. You and your champions killed Novati and her people. You cast neutrality aside and made it clear that you will seek the throne. Now you shirk from what must be done?"

"I didn't want to fight Novati. She forced me into it."

"We don't seek a battle with the princesses," Edra insisted, her otherwise smooth forehead lined with concern. "We mourn Princess Miar as much as you do. She was an honorable warrior and contributed to the stability of our people. We had a positive relationship with her."

"Is this what you'd support?" Drae flung her arm in Edra's direction in a dramatic gesture. "Weak cowards who hide behind others? It doesn't matter whether the rest of them knew or not. The fact that the others thought they could do such a thing tells us all we need to know. Do you think they would have punished them if they had succeeded? The Guardians want the power that belongs to us. We need to remove the threat."

No. The Shadows of Rurik and Cerin have one thing in common.

She shook her head. "I only kill people who target me. I don't do preemptive strikes. That's not my style."

"A weak human affectation." The other princess sneered. "Then maybe I will kill them myself."

Alison raised her arm and summoned a new shadow blade. "No. If we have to fight them later, we will, but not here and not now. Enough people have died today, including my friend, and she did that saving our asses. I won't dishonor her sacrifice because you're all hot and bothered to seize the throne."

Drae scoffed. "You side with the Guardians, then, Alison Brownstone?"

"I side with me for now," she responded coldly.

Novati's forces pivoted to face Drae's warriors, half of whom turned to face them. The others kept their attention on the Guardians' troops.

Alison pointed her blade at Drae. "It took tremendous power for that pyramid bomb. I suspect there were power magnification artifacts involved, and there's some evidence that your people were sniffing around for some recently. Maybe they weren't. Maybe you merely whispered in the right ears. Do you know what I think? My friend is dead and some of the people responsible have paid, but my guess is that the one most responsible is right in front of me. If you're so desperate to clear your enemies, then let's have another duel."

"A, no," Mason yelled in protest. "You're still—"

She silenced him with a glare.

"Only you and me, Drae, princess versus princess. If you want the throne so badly, you'll have to kill me eventually to get it."

Rasila raised her blade above her head. "I am Rasila, Princess of the Endless Shadow. I pledge my support to Alison Brownstone, Princess of the Shadow Forged, as the new queen of the Drow. I honor the fallen Princess Miar, and I will never offer my support to the weak Guardians who allowed such a cowardly assassination to occur. The blood of the Princess of the Soul Shadow is on their hands. Let Princess Alison and Princess Drae duel. Any who would dare to interfere will die at my hands."

Drae snorted and opened a portal. "I will not duel you, Princess of the Shadow Forged. Believe what you want, but also know that by not killing the Guardians, you've only made your own future more difficult." She finished with a thin smile. "Perhaps when this is all done, they'll agree to serve me and I won't need to kill them."

Her people backed slowly away from the other Drow warriors and headed toward the portal, never taking their eyes off their potential enemies.

Alison glared at her. "You're simply going to run? Who's the coward now?"

The other woman stepped toward her portal. "In a war, the only thing that matters is who wins. If you want to spill blood, do it, but today, I leave."

"This isn't over, Drae." She lowered her weapon. "If you've studied me at all, you know that. We Brownstones like to mind our own business until someone pushes us too far. Let me make this damned clear." She gestured to the princess and then to herself. "Whatever this is, it stays between Drow and handpicked allies. This is a Drow matter, not a matter between Drow and the Earth or the United States. If you make a move against my people on Earth, I will call everyone I know and we'll burn half of Oriceran to the ground, starting with everyone remotely associated with you."

"Are you threatening me?" Drae sounded amused. Her warriors began to retreat through the portal.

"I'm promising you," she stated icily. "You constantly say I'm not a true Drow. Well, it's time to keep this between Drow. If you don't care about me, care about King Oriceran's people and the US government."

"If you're so convinced you can raise armies to crush me, why not simply send them against me right away?"

She narrowed her eyes. "Because unlike you, I care when people die. I don't want a war."

Drae sighed, disappointment etched in her face. "And that's why you'll lose. You're too sentimental, an all too human trait." She stepped through the portal and it blinked closed.

Alison turned toward Edra. "Just because I don't support murdering you where you stand doesn't mean I trust any of you. Consider yourself warned."

"So you do intend to seek the throne?" Edra asked.

"For now, I'm going back to Earth. Remember everything I said to Drae. It applies to you, too." She gritted her teeth and took a breath to calm herself again. "My friend died today, and she didn't have to."

Rasila opened a portal directly in front of Alison's house. "I meant what I said, Alison."

"I know. Thanks for everything. It's only...Miar deserved better."

"On that, we both agree."

CHAPTER TWENTY-EIGHT

Rasila steepled her fingers in her lap and crossed her legs, comfortable on the high-backed chair in her sprawling receiving chamber. Lines of warriors stood on either side of her throne, their hands behind their back.

Quite unashamedly, she enjoyed the hint of fear she detected in the eyes of the Light Elf man standing in front of her. In the few days that had passed since Miar's death, she'd been busy consolidating her forces and doing her best to track both Drae's activities and that of the surviving Guardians. Now that the civil war had begun in earnest, she needed to be careful. A quick strike could end her life or Alison's. The princesses were powerful, but they weren't goddesses.

She had indeed meant everything she'd said and had long since stopped doubting Alison. Drae saw her human heritage as a weakness, but it had proven to be a strength again and again. Beyond her unusual mixture of magical abilities, she had gathered a large number of allies, not only her ridiculous monster of an adopted father. A Drow queen with such diverse resources would bring their people into the future.

All that made her wonder why a Light Elf representative wanted to meet with her.

"You've asked to speak to me, Avrik." She shrugged and pulled her hands apart. "So do it. I have better things to do than entertain a random Light Elf."

"I would like to speak to you alone," he replied.

Rasila whipped her wrist in a circle and gestured toward the door. Her warriors filed out of the room and closed the massive double doors to the chamber.

"Those who don't want others to hear what they have to say are often prepared to say something duplicitous and underhanded." She offered him a hungry grin. "Not that I inherently disapprove of such things."

"There are some among us who are prepared to support you," he explained. "A consolidation of the Drow leadership is best for stability. We could convince King Oriceran to recognize your claim, but this will require you to distance yourself from Alison Brownstone. She carries too much baggage because of her past actions and those of her father."

Rasila raised an eyebrow. "You want me to betray her after a public announcement of support?"

"No betrayal." He shook his head. "We understand certain things were handled poorly in the past with her, and King Oriceran was also angry with how these things were managed. We think, though, that Alison Brownstone is a disruptive element, and we don't want anything that risks disruption of the Great Treaty. A war among the Drow might lead to that."

"I don't know what Alison intends. I don't even believe she knows what she fully intends." She stood and a dark scowl settled over her face. "But I do know I don't care what outsiders have to say about Drow matters, especially Light Elves."

"Outsiders?" Avrik face scrunched in confusion. "She was born on Earth and didn't know about her heritage for most of her life. Aside from that, she's half-human."

She sliced her hand through the air in a defiant gesture. "She's half-Drow, and she is still the Princess of the Shadow Forged." She sauntered over to the Light Elf, a playful smile on her lips. "Don't worry. If she becomes queen, I suspect there will be less blood, not more."

"And if you're wrong?"

"Then attack us, Light Elf, and see the mighty armies of the Drow led by a powerful woman with equally powerful allies." Rasila licked her lips. "I'd be interested to see how many of you are worth one of us."

Avrik scoffed and shook his head slightly, the disgust plain. "You're not only risking the future of the Drow but you're risking the stability of Oriceran."

"How can I not? It's so deliciously entertaining."

Alison paced in her living room, her phone pressed to her ear. She'd put off talking to her father since returning from Oriceran but given his special role in the events leading up to the Guardians taking control, she could no longer pretend that he shouldn't be involved in the decision-making process.

"So that's where we're at," she finished. "Not everything played out as I expected. Some of Novati's people have approached me and made it clear they support me because I defeated her. Others support me because Rasila does. Others who were in Novati's faction don't support me, but they haven't openly declared against me either."

James grunted. "This shit sounds really complicated. Fuck."

"That's magical royal politics for you."

"When your mother died, you became the new Princess of the Shadow Forged. Doesn't that mean Novati has a daughter out there to replace her?"

She sighed. "Not that I know of. What little I know about the process suggests that some of her relatives will choose a new Princess of the Dark Sun from several candidates, but that will take a while. Since we're basically in the civil war already, I think they'll probably wait it out. It's the same situation for Miar's successor. Speaking of relatives, I also wonder if maybe you and Mom should take Thomas and lay low for a while."

He snorted. "Are you telling me you don't think we can protect your brother? You know we can take care of ourselves."

Alison rolled her eyes. "I'm saying you didn't sign up for more Drow shit. You're supposed to be retired, not worrying about stupid shape-changing assassins again, especially when you have a new baby to worry about."

"Fuck that," he retorted. "If you want me to stay out of this because you think it'll cause more trouble, I'll stay out of it. But if you need me to come there and do my thing, I will. I don't care if that means I waste every fucking Drow on Oriceran. I've whipped their asses before and I'll do it again."

Alison chuckled. "I think that might start a war of the worlds, Dad."

"So? It's not like I haven't done that before. I don't give a shit about Oriceran or the Great Treaty. I only care about my family and my friends. If that means they need to be reminded of what I can do when I'm pissed off, I'll do that. Whispy would love it if we really dropped the chains."

She grimaced and stopped her pacing. Her dad pissed off and at full power wasn't something she ever wanted to see.

"No, Dad. I love you and I appreciate that you're willing to blow up a country on my behalf—or maybe even a planet—but I think the best strategy, for now, is to keep this contained to the Drow as much as possible."

"You told me you had Mason, Hana, and Drysi helping you," James countered.

"I did, and I wonder if that was a mistake. Now that I have Drow forces, it might be best to only use them. Every outsider I include only increases the chance that other outsiders get involved, and then we're talking about shit getting out of hand." She walked over to a window and stared out at the calm water. "I need to give them a reason to not intervene. My mom tried to walk away from her responsibilities, and I don't blame her for that given what a psycho Laena was. But now, it's my responsibility to not walk away. I can save lives here. Maybe a lot of lives."

"You'll have to kill some people to do that. You do know that?"

Alison placed a hand on the window. Everything about

the outside of her home was calm and peaceful. No one would think a princess waging war lived there.

"I don't regret facing Novati," she replied. "Even if I'm half-convinced Drae set the whole thing up."

"Do you think she'll target you on Earth?" James asked.

She lowered her hand. "Not until she's ready for the kill. I'll say this for that sneaky bitch, she's damned careful. She knows the only thing holding me in check is that I don't want unnecessary deaths, but if she did have anything to do with that assassination attempt, I owe her for Miar and I will kill her."

He grunted. "So what are you gonna do?"

"What Brownstones do best. Kick ass."

The front door opened, and Mason stepped inside holding a paper bag.

"I have to go, Dad. Mason's back with my sushi."

James chuckled. "Eat first. Kick ass later. It sounds like me."

CHAPTER TWENTY-NINE

A slight breeze shifted the fragments of glass on the ground and produced a soft tinkle. The sound was almost musical. It'd been a couple of weeks since the deaths of Miar and Novati. Alison had attended a surprisingly modest funeral the previous week, but she wanted to pay her respects at the actual location of her friend's sacrifice.

Friend. The word was laden with meaning. They'd spent far more time together in recent months, and she'd convinced herself before that Miar was only a Drow ally. But now that the woman was dead, she realized it was more than that.

Rasila stepped through the strewn fragments and they crunched under her boots. "I'll be honest, Alison. I'm not so sure we shouldn't have made our move right then and there. This doesn't end any other way than with Drae dead. The Guardians might do the right thing and surrender, but she needs to die. Even if she didn't have anything to do with the plots against you, she is a horrid woman."

Alison crouched and picked up one of the fragments. Although it looked like frosted glass, it still radiated magic and was warm to the touch.

"Even if we assume the Guardians and all their people are acceptable losses, you're still talking about starting a major fight in an area with too many innocent people. And we wouldn't be talking about a normal fight. We both know the level of power necessary to eliminate a princess." She nodded toward the crater in the distance. "And if Drae has been collecting artifacts to set up death traps, she might have had a few other tricks up her sleeve. The risk of collateral damage was simply too high."

"Most wars end with the blood of innocents spilled," the other woman pointed out. "The only choice we have is to end it as quickly as possible to minimize that risk. And you should know, this is now a war. Whether Drae manipulated the situation or not, she is our immediate enemy, and she is too much of a devious coward to ever agree to something as straightforward as Novati."

She stood. "Do you think she somehow pushed Novati into threatening me? I've wondered that a fair amount lately."

"I think there was a confluence of events, and she was the one most poised to benefit from them. It's as they say on Earth. Always ask yourself—*Cui bono?*" Rasila inhaled deeply through her nose. "Do you know what I hate most about Earth?"

Alison startled, taken off-guard by the sudden change in topic. "Long lines at the movies?"

"The smell."

"The smell?" She laughed. "Is this the part where you reveal you're a sadistic artificial intelligence program?"

Rasila frowned at her. "What are you talking about?"

"Have you never seen *The Matrix*? The movie? It's a classic. Plus, ever since Keanu admitted he was a Light Elf, certain things about his career make sense. It's too bad he stopped making movies when the gates opened."

The other princess scoffed. "I have little use for human movies, let alone human movies starring disguised Light Elves."

"Never mind. The point is that Earth doesn't smell bad." She shrugged.

"It's not that it smells bad," the other Drow countered. "It smells different, and it's the first thing I noticed. At first, I thought it was only the cities, but even the wilderness areas smell so foreign."

"Is there a point to all this?"

Rasila smiled. "I spend time on Earth because it is helpful and provides resources, but Oriceran is my home, and I'm willing to do what it takes to protect that home and the Drow. Drae will not be straightforward. Even now, I have no idea where she is. This means we will need to employ commensurate tactics to defeat her." She held a hand up. "I'm not saying we need to be cowardly, but a little sneakiness might not hurt."

Alison frowned. "I'm not saying I'm above misdirection, but I won't sink to her level."

"Then I'll do what I need to without you knowing." Her companion's smile turned mischievous.

She winced. "I don't know if that makes me feel any better."

"War isn't something one can wage without getting one's hands dirty, Alison." Rasila shook her head. Concern lined her features. "If you don't believe that, you should renounce your claim right now."

"I know." She sighed. "But I want to play this as direct as I can."

"I understand that, and I also understand why you believe it." She gestured around the fragment piles. "The Guardians might have given up the faction that attempted the assassination, but whether they came up with that plan themselves or Drae somehow manipulated them into it, they're now desperate. That means they might try something even more foolish. They understand all too well how precarious their hold on power is now that the princesses have begun to move."

"Then keep an eye on them. I won't kill them unless I know for certain they're attacking me. I thought I made that clear. And if you support me, I don't want you doing that either."

Rasila exhaled a disappointed sigh. "You make everything more difficult than it needs to be." She raised a finger. "Ah, and I almost forgot to tell you. A Light Elf approached me and suggested his little group could convince King Oriceran to recognize me as the rightful heir to the throne."

Irritation flashed through Alison, followed by resignation. Of course the Light Elves would be concerned about the state of Drow succession for all the reasons she was.

"I'll be honest, Rasila," she murmured. "I'm not prepared to wage war against the Light Elves too. If you have their support, I'd probably back off. I would have no choice."

Her friend shook her head. "The Drow need a queen. This recent farce with the Guardians only proves that, but we've been static for too long. You will usher us into the future."

"But I'm still not sure I want to be queen."

Rasila snickered. "You say that, but your actions scream that you do. I won't resist if you clear the path for me, but until I am seated on the throne, I will proceed with the assumption that you will be queen."

Alison should have told her the idea was ridiculous. A half-human who grew up on Earth had no business being the Drow queen, but for the first time in a while, she couldn't bring herself to say the words.

The other princess had been correct. Alison had half-thought of the Guardians as some kind of plucky freedom fighters. She had assumed that with the toppling of the tyrant, something approaching democracy might take hold among the Drow, but even a cursory examination of Earth history proved that removing a tyrant was a necessary but not sufficient step for democracy and freedom.

I've been naïve. This isn't Earth, and the Drow won't form the United States of Drow. If the Guardians are already launching murderous assassination plans that kill dozens of people, they won't get better as time passes. Many of them have had hundreds of years to think about this kind of thing.

Rasila raised a palm. Several dark tentacles rose from the center and disappeared after a few seconds. "In either case," she explained, "Drae must be taken care of. I assume you can agree, without reservation, that she's not fit to be queen. She's not even at Laena's level." She snorted. "If anything, she reminds me of the Widowmaker. And to be clear, when I say she must be taken care of, that means she has to die." She locked gazes with her friend and challenged her to dare to suggest otherwise.

Finally, Alison nodded slowly. "She had her chance to do this peacefully. She wants a fight so we'll give her one."

The other woman's dour expression vanished and was replaced by an easy smile. "I look forward to fighting at your side again."

CHAPTER THIRTY

Drae circled the life-sized image of Laena slowly. Her spell had conjured it in the center of the small hexagonal chamber. Unlike the withered crone imprisoned by the Guardians, the beautiful, smooth-skinned woman before her stood in resplendent armor so dark it seemed to swallow the light. An ornate crown of sharp horns rested atop her head. After a few more seconds of appreciation, the princess offered a smile to the Drow man standing in the corner of the room

"You were key to recent events, Marat," she murmured to him. "I know you have your doubts, but you chose well in serving me. Novati would have repeated the mistakes of Laena. She would have weakened our people, and we're stronger now that she is gone."

He nodded although he looked to the side as if ashamed of betraying his former mistress. Drae didn't mind. She preferred that a spark burned in his heart. A guilty conscience presented another string she could tug to control a puppet.

"Everything went as planned," she murmured. "I had some concerns that the Guardians might not do what I wanted, but they reacted exactly as I had planned. Everything is proceeding as I have foreseen."

Marat frowned. "You anticipated that Alison Brownstone would defeat Novati?"

"I couldn't be sure but I suspected that would be the case." She continued to peer at the image of Laena. "Novati's greatest talent has always been boasting, and the Princess of the Shadow Forged might be young, but her adult life has been forged in a crucible of near-constant battle. It doesn't matter. Every new encounter I push her into, I better learn the limits of her abilities. The feeble human wizard faction I sacrificed in Russia was as useful for that as Novati."

He swallowed, clearly disturbed by her ruthless machinations. Again, she didn't care. Fear was also a useful tool.

"I…you could have died, Princess. You let the artifacts charge well beyond your original plan."

Drae approached the Laena image and stared into her static eyes. "It was necessary to dispose of either Rasila or Miar. I'm not dissatisfied with the results, even if I couldn't goad the Princess of the Shadow Forged into eliminating the Guardians." Her nostrils flared. "The other princesses think themselves so brave. They are coarse and don't understand that there are different ways to show courage."

She stepped away from the image and nodded, satisfied. "Laena's the key to my next step. Striking at the Princess of the Shadow Forged directly on Earth isn't possible, not until I've consolidated control. She's proven far more resilient than I would have expected. I'm not surprised, but it does present difficulties and now, I've lost the use of Novati as a shield. Miar's people have pledged themselves to the other two princesses, and even Rasila's followers accept her as subordinate to the Princess of the Shadow Forged. Amusingly, the refusal to kill the Guardians might actually work out better for my plan."

Marat cupped his chin as he thought about what Drae had explained. "How does it work better? Most of the Guardians survived."

"But now, every Drow knows that their brethren were involved in an assassination plot. The population is split and fewer support them. What good is it to have a whole council of cowards who play at assassinations? They say we might as well bring Laena back."

"But isn't the situation now more precarious?" He frowned. "You've done well to predict everyone's reactions, Princess, but that was when things hadn't changed. Now, there's nothing but chaos."

Drae wasn't about to admit to her brief worry that she'd miscalculated. She hadn't realized that Novati's warriors would so immediately and instinctively side with Alison. Even if some of them had reconsidered it with the later passage of time, the risk of the half-Drow coming back to Oriceran and gathering more Drow to her side was too great. The damned half-breed possessed an annoying ability to turn enemies into friends. Rasila's pledge of loyalty was proof of that.

Unlike Alison, Drae would rule through fear and manipulation. Those took work to maintain. Brownstone garnered love and respect, and those fed themselves. They spread like an infection.

I will defeat you, Alison Brownstone. I am a full Drow and you're a half-breed mistake. It's my destiny to destroy you. I will kill you and point your beast of a father on a false path.

"No," she muttered. "Chaos breeds opportunities. Sacrifices must be made, and the great queen Laena will arise one last time to serve her people."

She smiled, but her heart thumped hard and she didn't like what she was feeling. It was unfamiliar and disgusting. A princess of the Drow should never feel it.

Damn you, Alison Brownstone, for making me afraid of you.

Drow succession is heating up and Alison is in the crosshairs. It's time to solve the problem… for good. Join Alison and her crew as they handle challengers thrown her way in *Drow Triumphant.*

Get sneak peeks, exclusive giveaways, behind the scenes content, and more.
PLUS you'll be notified of special **one day only fan pricing** on new releases.

Sign up today to get free stories.

CLICK HERE

or visit: https://marthacarr.com/read-free-stories/

I spent last weekend in Chicago hanging out with Fans. Pictures are posted in the Facebook Fan group and it was a blast! Big Thank You to Randy Barber for organizing everything. There was even a fan lunch the week before in New York City and now, there's talk of a bigger scene – Martha Con!

If you want to know more come hang out with us in the Fan group and message Randy. We're looking at doing a big D&D game but using Oriceran characters instead. If it's in Austin, there's talk of a tour of all the bars that Leira Berens or Maggie Parker or even Yumfuck and Hagan have hung out in.

That's right – all the places mentioned in both The Leira Chronicles and The Adventures of Maggie Parker actually exist. The barbeque at The Mean Eyed Cat is amazing. If you stop by there, try the brisket nachos but bring an appetite. We had a fan lunch there not too long ago, complete with fan Debi Sateren in the peapod costume she won! Outside is that 400-year-old tree I mentioned, the hub of the world. The new owners of the bar wanted to tear down the 100-plus year-old building, but the tree saved the day.

If it happens, this will be created by the Fans and for the Fans, and we'll see who might drop by to say hello too. More on that later but feel free to reach out to Randy if you have ideas or enthusiasm.

While I was in Chicago, I also spent time hanging with my tribe of women. It was yet again a good reminder that no matter where I wander I have roots that go deep with this wonderful group of women who show up at a moment's notice with a dish in hand, a warm, long hug and share laughs and hard stories and a solid belief in each other's dreams. It really doesn't get better than that.

We were gathered to celebrate birthdays, new jobs, and other milestones – and a very special request for me to become the wonderful Izzie's godmother. Izzie is an almost fourteen year old powerhouse that I have hung with since she was four and we went to the movies together or played in the park. Back then, her greatest ambition was to play lead guitar in a rock band. We had come together to pass along whatever wisdom we had as a group to her, and to let her know that not just me, but all of us were there for her – no matter what. Imagine if we had all had that kind of support as young teenagers from such a wild bunch of badassery women pursuing their dreams shoulder to shoulder? I'm just glad and forever grateful to be with them now. May we all find our tribe. More adventures to follow.

Thank you for not only reading this book, but these author notes in the back.

Author notes are different for every author, and every time. Sometimes, I might just modify and add to the author notes of my collaborator. A couple of times, I forget until it's too late to plug them into a book.

Once or twice I might have made shit up (anyone remember the lawn faires?)

Those were some serious assholes.

Here, I'm just going to do a very small scene of very large importance.

The man shivered in the cold, the snow slowly melting against his Doc Martens. His dark green jacket doing nothing to help him stand out in the early morning darkness. The only light was from the orange embers he was coaxing back to life.

"Dammit," he put his hands up to his mouth,

blowing hard to warm them up. He eyed the logs and moved his head back and forth, considering what he needed to do next.

Turning around, he grabbed two axe hewn logs and laid them down, nestling them into the embers. "That should do it." He nodded once before turning around to head back into his man-den out back of the house.

His wife didn't like him preparing the meats in her kitchen, too much white in there.

Stomping in the snow he made it up to his old garage, stomped his feet before pushing open the door and going inside with a squeak as the door shut behind him.

He looked over the spices laid out on his table, grabbing a bit of cumin. Turning the brisket over, he tossed the spice on the back side. He looked up, eyeing the black and white picture of the winning bbq team from last year, keeping the defeat fresh in his mind.

He sniffed the meat, trying to tell if he had the spices right before cleaning his hands and then ripping off a large sheet of aluminum foil.

"This is the day I figure out how to beat you, Brownstone." He muttered, wrapping up the first bit of meat. "And then I'll stomp you into the ground with beef, pork and poultry."

Just so you know, BBQ can be Life.

Ad Aeternitatem,

Michael Anderle

OTHER BOOKS BY MARTHA CARR

THE WITCH NEXT DOOR

OTHER BOOKS BY JUDITH BERENS

OTHER BOOKS BY MARTHA CARR

JOIN THE ORICERAN UNIVERSE FAN GROUP ON FACEBOOK!

BOOKS BY MICHAEL ANDERLE

For a complete list of books by Michael Anderle, please visit

www.lmbpn.com/ma-books/

All LMBPN Audiobooks are Available at Audible.com and iTunes. For a complete list of audiobooks visit:

www.lmbpn.com/audible